Witch of the Glens

Witch
of the Glens

By SALLY WATSON

Drawings by Barbara Werner

74872   THE VIKING PRESS

New York

To my favorite witch and *uruisg*
Jean and Don
and their two small kelpies
Kathy and Mark

Contents

8 Contents

Gaelic Terms

Amadain (masculine, *amadan*). Fool.

Briosag. Witch, sorceress.

Chlanna nan con, thigibh a sh's gheibh sibh feoil. "Sons of the dogs, come hither, and you shall have flesh" (Cameron war cry).

Dhia dhuit. A greeting ("good day," literally, "God to-day").

Droch-inntinneach. Evil-minded.

Dubh (also *dhu*). Black.

Each uisghe. Water horse (mythical sea-monster, probably with some connection to the Loch Ness Monster, which has been seen frequently for at least 1500 years and to which Saint Columba of Iona gave a good scolding in 565, as recorded by the Abbot of Iona).

Filleadh mor. The great-plaid, kilt and plaid in one piece. (The plaid, or plaidie, was worn around the shoulders and sometimes over the head.)

Ghillie. An attendant or follower of a clan chief or chieftain.

Kelpie. A water witch.

Mallaichte. Wicked.

M'eudain. An endearment.

Mise-an-dhuit. An exclamation (literally, "Me today!").

Mo chridhe. An endearment (literally, "My heart").

Mo thruigh. An exclamation (literally, "My sorrow!").

Mor (or *mhor*). Great, large.

Nathrach. Serpent.

Seach. Interjection: "Yes?" "Well—" "Truly!" "Really?"

Sgian dhu. Black knife: a small dagger usually worn in the top of the right stocking by men, just below the knee on the outside, where it is most convenient to reach.

Slaoightire. Scoundrel.

Uruisg (plural, *uruisgean*). A hobgoblin; sometimes thought to be half human, half hobgoblin. A most disagreeable fellow, in any case.

Pronouncing Gaelic

Gaelic pronunciation is in some ways totally different from English. For instance, *s* in front of *i* or *e* sounds like *sh; th, bh, dh,* and *gh* are sometimes (but not always) silent; *mh* is usually pronounced *v;* and *ch* has a sound not found in English at all, and made by trying to say *kh* as far back in the throat as possible.

Following are the pronunciations for some of the names and words found in this book:

dubh—doo

each uisghe—ekh oosh-ga ("oo" as in "look")

Eithne—Ay-na

Ewen—Yew-en

ghillie—gilly

Hamish—Hay-mish

Ian—Ee-an

Lachlan—Lakh-lan

Loch Leven—Lokh Leeven

Mairi—Mah-ri

mhor—vore

mo chridhe—mo cree

Seumas—Shay-mas (James)

sgian dhu—skean doo

uruisg—oorishk

Historical Note

To avoid confusion I have in this book described clan tartans more or less as they exist today. This is not strictly accurate. To begin with, in 1644 clans had not yet adopted specific tartans to be worn by all their members, and probably none of the tartans were the same, in either pattern or color, as they are today. In fact, it is very difficult to

know just what they did look like, for all kinds of vegetable dyes were used, and the remnants of old tartans
that we find today are so faded and changed in color that
they seem mostly gray or gray-brown, and it is hard to tell
what colors they once were.

Witch of the Glens

THE PART OF
SCOTLAND
WHERE KELPIE'S
ADVENTURE
TOOK
PLACE

1. The Gypsies

THE people of Inverness were deeply annoyed. A number of them stood in the square and scowled with great hostility at the three tattered wanderers in their midst—but their anger held a wary quality.

"Tinklers! Gypsies!" they cried accusingly, and the soft, sibilant sound of the Gaelic was less soft but more sibilant than usual. *"Briosag!"* ("Witch!") muttered some with conviction but caution. "Thieves!" they added, getting to the real heart of the annoyance. And with this fresh reminder of their grievances they began picking up stones as they advanced toward the man, woman, and girl.

Anyone who expected to see clan loyalty in this gypsy family would have been terribly disappointed. The massive bent shoulders and stringy legs of the man somehow evaporated between two houses, and the final glance from his pasty dark face was one of hooded derision.

Old Mina Faw didn't seem at all put out by her man's

desertion. One might have thought she had expected it. Her scrawny figure seemed to grow taller as she turned a once-handsome hag face toward the crowd, and her sunken pale eyes flashed. The crowd hesitated. Everyone knew Old Mina was a witch, with the most devastating Evil Eye in all Scotland.

But surprisingly Mina chose to pacify them. After all, there weren't many towns in the Highlands in this year of 1644, and it was well not to be alienating those few too deeply. "Och, now!" She wheedled the crowd in her thin but powerful voice. "Ye wouldn't be wishing to harm a poor old woman, now, would ye?"

It wasn't at all that they weren't wishing to harm her. But no one wanted to risk having his hands fall off or his cattle die. They regarded her dubiously, making up their minds. "Witch!" repeated someone from the safety of the back. "Thief!" cried several more with fresh indignation, and they began to move forward again.

"Thief?" echoed Mina indignantly. "Not I! I would only be reading your palms and telling good fortune for ye. If anyone has been lifting your belongings, it must be my wicked wee Kelpie, whom I am beating every night for her sins." And she pointed accusingly at an undersized goblin-lass who might have been perhaps fifteen or seventeen years old, dressed in an outrageous assortment of faded scraps. Long black elf-locks flapped about her thin face and down her back. Eyes that were not quite canny peered out like those of an alarmed wee beast—or a witch.

The "wicked wee Kelpie" didn't stay to dispute the issue. With one bright, mutinous glance at Mina, she dived through the startled fringe of the crowd like a young stoat and ran away into the narrow steep lanes of the town.

The Inverness crowd promptly forgot Mina and took after the lass. "Thief!" they yelled with new enthusiasm. And whatever was convenient to pick up, they threw.

It was fortunate that Kelpie was experienced in this sort of thing, for it was a nasty chase, and she knew all too well what might happen if they caught her. With cunning amounting to sheer genius she ran and dodged, doubled back and forth between houses, wriggled over and under and around obstacles. Now and then her intense small face broke into a pointed grin of appreciation at her own cleverness—for there was something exhilarating in outwitting an entire town—but very real fear lurked behind those uncanny blue eyes. To tell the truth, it was the tide of ill will surging behind her which oppressed her even more than the stones. But Kelpie did not realize this, for she was so used to ill will that she could not remember anything else.

As for Mina's deplorable behavior, Kelpie was annoyed but not in the least astonished. Mina had merely followed the law of self-preservation, the only law Kelpie knew.

She herself would do the same thing, given the chance. It was the only way to stay alive.

"*Briosag!* Witch!"

Kelpie swerved round a corner and wished that she *were* a witch. If so, she wouldn't be running now but putting a braw spell on them all, causing their legs to buckle under them and stay that way for three days too, so that the whole town would be crawling about on hands and knees, just— She laughed at the picture and took another corner at full speed. Just wait until she *was* a witch! Och, no one would chase her then, or beat her, either. . . .

A red petticoat spread on a gorse bush vanished magically as she flew past. Why not? If she got away, she was a petticoat richer. If not, what would it be mattering, a petticoat more, since she already had two stolen purses, a kerchief, and a fine *sgian dhu* on her anyhow?

Up hill and down and around, and finally away out of the town, and presently the stones ceased to bite at her ankles and back, and the yells were lost behind. Her breath seared her lungs now, and she hurtled down the hill toward the river which led from Loch Ness to Moray Firth. At last she threw herself into a cold, wet, but safely thick bank of broom, bracken, and juniper, where she lay panting and gasping painfully. Mina and Bogle would be safely away by now and waiting for her down along the path that was the only road along Loch Ness. Let them wait. She had earned a rest. She was sore bruised and aching from the stones, and her bare feet, tough as they were, hurt from the cobbled streets of the town.

Och, she thought pleasantly, if only they would some day be catching and hanging Mina, and Bogle too—but only, of course, after Kelpie had learned all the witchcraft that Mina knew, and perhaps more. Oh, to be a more powerful witch than Mina, and to be putting all kinds of curses on her until all scores were settled!

Curled up in her nest of bracken, head resting on the scarlet petticoat, Kelpie drifted into her favorite daydream. *Dhé,* how Mina would plead for mercy! Her arms and legs would shrivel up, just, and her few remaining teeth fall out. Kelpie smiled, looking like a starry-eyed lass dreaming of romance. Then her short upper lip curled and lifted, revealing a row of small, sharp white teeth, so that she looked more like a wolf cub dreaming of dinner.

The long northern twilight was beginning to creep into the Great Glen, for sunlight vanished early in the valley between those high, steep, massive hills, even in March. She must go on now, or she would be beaten for delaying. And presently, still sore, she was loping silently down the path by the loch, where new gorse and bracken grew between patches of old snow. Two or three miles down she met Bogle and Mina sitting on their bundles and waiting.

"You have taken your time about getting here," said Bogle. "And how many purses were you taking?"

Twilight had deepened into the toneless half-light of
gloaming. Light had slowly drained from the Glen, leaving a world of eerie gray on the hill above Loch Ness. The
loch itself was liquid iron, from which might easily arise
the three black humps and snaky neck of the *each uisghe*,
the water horse who lived there. A meager supper was
over, and the only color left in the world was the small
salmon-pink pennant of cloud flying over the black shoulder of Meall Fuarvounie and reflected in the shining
crystal ball in Mina's hand.

She spread a shabby bit of stolen black velvet on the
springy turf and set the crystal sphere lovingly in the exact
center. "And now you will be reading the glass with me,"
she said.

It was a nightly ritual. Ordinarily Kelpie found it interesting, exciting, but tonight she was sore and aching and
rebellion was in her. It was foolish, of course, to express
such feelings. It was to risk not only a beating—which,
being used to, she did not fear—but an evil spell, which
she did. But she expressed them now and then, all the
same.

"May the *uruisg* be away with you!" she said sweetly
and ducked. Mina's fist merely caught the top of Kelpie's
tangled head, but her snarl was more effective.

"Mind me so!" Her voice rasped. "And how do you
think to be learning witchcraft else?"

"I am reading the crystal with you every night," muttered Kelpie. "But you'll never let me be trying alone, and you've taught me never so much as a single wee spell."

"And listen to her now!" The hateful voice was a croak of derision, echoed by a snort from the bulky gray shadow that was Bogle. "She cannot crawl yet and she is wanting to run!" And this time the blow fell on Kelpie's high, thin cheekbone before she could think to duck. "Look into the crystal, *amadain!*"

Kelpie considered further defiance and then decided against it. She didn't really feel up to another beating tonight, and she did want to learn witchcraft. So she permitted Mina's long gnarled hand to clutch her own so that Kelpie would be able to see what Mina did. For a seer could share his sight with another by touching him, and Kelpie, said Mina, was not yet ready to see alone. Night after night, for as long as she could remember, Kelpie had looked into the ball with Mina, describing what she saw, while the old woman questioned and corrected her.

"Now," said Mina, and Kelpie stared into the luminous ball. First it clouded, then the center began to glow dully, and then a vague picture developed. Kelpie's dark head bent forward on its long neck, and her eyes grew wide and fixed. . . .

Two young men were riding along a loch-side on fine horses, with a blond giant behind them on a shaggy Highland pony. Bright tartan *filleadh mór*—the bulky great-

kilts—beat heavily against their thighs and swung over
their shoulders, and their heads were high with the proud
confidence of the well-born.

Kelpie recognized one of them. Young Glenfern, it was,
whose father was a minor chieftain of Clan Cameron, and
who had once given her a farthing and a sudden compas-
sionate smile that lit his grave dark-eyed face like sunshine. The smile had roused in Kelpie a strange sensation
of joy and resentment combined, and the feeling came
back now as she stared. There was gladness behind the
composure of his face as he rode, and his dark shoulder-
length hair lifted in the breeze. And Kelpie, ignorant of
the eternal attraction of lad for lass, frowned at the pleasant pain of her own feelings. She spared no more than a
glance for the other young man in MacDonald tartan,
whose narrow face seemed composed of straight lines,
whose freckles matched the blaze of his red hair, whose
expression seemed to laugh at all the world.

"Who is that?" muttered Mina, peering. "What will
they be to us? Do you know them?"

"No," lied Kelpie, whose policy was to deceive Mina
and Bogle whenever possible, just on principle.

"I would be seeing something of the King, or the war,
or Mac Cailein Mor," said Mina fretfully.

Kelpie spared her a narrow, speculative glance. Why
was Mina so interested of late in politics? Of what benefit
to her was the blaze of civil war sweeping through the

remote world of England and even the less remote world
of the Lowlands? As far as Kelpie could see, it affected
them not at all—except, of course, that Mac Cailein Mor,
Marquis of Argyll, Chief of Clan Campbell, was head of
the Covenant army of the Lowlands and therefore a
merciless hunter of witches. But then Mac Cailein Mor
came into these Western Highlands only now and then,
and merely to wipe out here and there a few of the clans
whom he had always hated. A terrible fierce enemy he
was, no doubt, and one deserving the Evil Eye—but
what was he to Mina, at all?

"Is it still the lads riding, then?" Mina persisted. "And
who will they be, whatever?"

Always and always Kelpie must describe every detail,
just as if Mina couldn't see for herself. Kelpie was irri-
tated. "How should I be knowing?" she snapped, and a
blow on the ear set her head ringing.

"Don't know! *Amadain!* What tartan will they be wearing?"

It was too much. Kelpie jerked away, too angry to care
about the consequences. "*Nathrach!*" She spat. "Look for
yourself!"

The motionless gray bulk in the shadows now stirred
and gave a low, spiteful chuckle. "She cannot," Bogle
said, wheezing with satisfaction. "It is sure I am now; her
Sight will be going from her. It was for that, these long
years ago, that she must be stealing a wee bairn with the

ringed eyes of the Second Sight, and holding her hand so
that she can see through other eyes what she cannot see
for herself—"

There was a scream of fury from old Mina, and a bat-
tered saucepan hurtled through the dusk, hit Bogle's
ragged shoulder, and fell into the heather. Bogle chuckled
with malicious triumph. It wasn't that he hated Mina in
particular. He was quite impartial, was Bogle; he simply
hated all mankind and greatly enjoyed seeing anyone unhappy. Now he ducked his head slightly and shook with
laughter as the saucepan was followed by an assortment
of sticks, stolen objects, and curses.

Kelpie sat perfectly still. A universe of startling possi-
bilities was opening to her mind—because, with Mina's
hand no longer touching hers, the tiny picture in the
crystal glowed more sharply, brightly clear than she had
ever seen it.

Wrapped in her tattered plaidie in a nest of last year's
dry bracken, she lay awake after the long gloaming had
deepened to black and stars peeped out to grow dim again
as the unearthly white radiance of the northern lights—
the Dancers—shimmered and pulsed over the western
hills. The wonder of the lights, as Kelpie watched, seemed
to match the wonder in her heart.

Had Bogle told the truth? Mina's behavior made Kelpie

think he had. And it was certain that the crystal was even clearer for her without Mina's touch.

So then, was it also true that she had been stolen? From where? Kelpie reached back into her memory but could find nothing but the vagrant life of gypsies—tramping, begging, stealing, telling fortunes and selling spells and charms in the Highlands, running from witch-hunters in the Lowlands, sleeping under the sky.

Och, how could she ever be finding out? Only, perhaps, by becoming a greater witch than Mina and putting the power upon her. And indeed, it was a great advantage if Mina no longer had the Sight! *Dhé,* but she had other powers, had Mina, terrible powers of cursing and spells! She was clever, too, and for all her age she used a stick with great strength. Kelpie must be canny, she must so. The cold streams of the northern lights faded, and when they were gone, Kelpie was asleep.

2. The Waif

IT was one of those days that couldn't decide between winter and spring. A cold, gusty wind whistled thinly through dark pine and barren birch and chased fat clouds over the sky one by one, causing flurries of hard rain to alternate with pale and hesitant sunshine.

They had traveled the thirty miles of Loch Ness, stopping at the village near Urquhart Castle, and again at Kilcummin, where they had nearly been caught picking the purse of one of the MacDonald chieftains. And now they were moving south beside the silver ripples of Loch Lochy.

Kelpie was far ahead of Mina and Bogle, moving along high on the hillside with a prancing motion caused partly by high spirits and partly by the masses of tough-stemmed heather that covered the slope. She was still sore from her latest beating, and also hungry. Her life consisted largely of pain and hunger and cold, and was peopled by enemies to be feared and hated or fools to be tricked, but Kelpie had discovered all that long ago and was quite used to the fact and found life very enjoyable anyway. Certainly it was never dull, and she had a zest for adventure.

And in spite of everything, the world was beautiful. Kelpie could forgive it a lot for that. In any case, her day was coming! She had deliberately described the details in last night's crystal quite wrongly, and Mina hadn't known.

Or had she?

This appalling thought caused Kelpie to miss her usually sure footing and to step right in the middle of a gorse bush. Neither the travel-hardened toughness of the bare brown foot nor the deceptive beauty of the silvery leaves saved her from a good pricking, and Kelpie swore with an ardent fluency that would have pleased Bogle greatly. Still hopping and cursing, she saw the movement and color of the three horsemen down the loch much later than she should have. They were coming along toward her in the path below and doubtless had well-filled purses which might well be lightened. She was halfway down the steep slope when suddenly the sun shone brightly from behind the latest cloud, and Kelpie recognized the scene from the crystal: young Glenfern and his redhaired companion and the giant blond *ghillie* riding behind.

But there was no time to wonder about it. Timing her

movements carefully, Kelpie threw herself headlong down
the last steep bank and sprawled full length in the path,
almost under the horses' feet.

"*Dhé!*" exclaimed Ian Cameron as he and Alex reined
the horses so sharply that they reared for a moment on
their hind legs. All he could see on the ground was a pitifully small and tattered figure, clearly in great danger of
being trampled to death.

Alex MacDonald, from his better position behind, saw
something a little more. As Ian's horse stepped alarmingly
close to Kelpie, one "thin and helpless" arm moved, neatly
and efficiently, the precise six inches required for safety.
Alex's red eyebrows arched, and an appreciative grin
danced on his face. He relaxed and prepared to enjoy the
comedy that was sure to follow.

The crisis was over in a moment. "Is it all right you
are?" demanded Ian of the wee figure, and the wee figure
nodded biting its lip in a fine imitation of silent courage
as it raised itself painfully to an elbow. For Kelpie had
discovered that this sort of act was much more touching
than loud wails and tears. She decided to have a hurt
back, this being hard to disprove, as well as more impres-
sive than other hurts. So she winced to indicate great pain
and looked up with a brave and pathetic smile.

The lads looked back at her. A scrawny waif it was,
tattered and unbelievably dirty. The tangled dark hair,
apparently never touched by water or comb, fell over the

thin face in a way that reminded Ian of shaggy Highland cattle—except that these eyes were unlike those of any cattle that ever lived. They were long and black-fringed, set at a slant in the narrow face, and strangely ringed. Around each black pupil was a wide circle of smoky blue, then a narrow one of lightish gray, and a third of deep and vivid blue. Astonishing eyes, almost alarming! Where had he seen them before?

While Ian stared in wonder and pity, Alex made a few further observations of his own. He noted the high cheekbones and the pointed chin and the wicked slant of black brows and the short upper lip—giving rather the effect, thought Alex, of a wicked elfin creature, or perhaps a witch. Amused but wary, he sat back and let his foster brother make up his mind. Ian wouldn't have been noticing, of course, that the wee *briosag* threw herself into the path on purpose. Ian had the way of always believing the best of everyone.

Ian was aware of the cynical smile behind him. A nasty suspicious mind Alex had! It was a pity. What else could he be expecting of a poor wild waif like this? What sort of life must she have had? Then Ian remembered where he had seen her before: with that wicked old witch Mina. Och, the poor creature!

" 'Tis hurt you are," he said worriedly, to Kelpie's relief. She had feared for a moment that she'd been too subtle altogether.

"Och, only a little," she whispered, putting on a braw show of dreadful pain heroically borne.

"Now, do not be overdoing it," drawled Alex.

Kelpie shot him a look which, had she been a properly qualified witch, would surely have caused him to break out with every loathsome disease known to mankind. Unfortunately the only effect of her venomous glare was that Alex's smile broadened to an insulting chuckle. Och, what a beast he was, then, with the bony, freckled, jeering face of him, and the two jaunty tufts of red hair jutting upward just where horns ought to sprout! She was about to tell him so, and in great detail, but just in time she remembered her role and Ian, who was still showing his pity and dismay.

What a misfortune, he thought, that this should happen now, just when he and Alex were nearly home again after those long months away in Oxford, where he had been savagely homesick. They were about to get home early, and with very important news, and now this had to happen, not five miles from Glenfern.

"What shall we be doing with you at all?" he said. "We cannot just be leaving her here!" he added fiercely, turning on Lachlan, the blond *ghillie*, who, looking larger than usual on his short shaggy pony, had muttered something from behind.

"Give her a copper," Alex said, laughing, "and see how quickly she'll mend!"

Copper indeed! thought Kelpie. It was silver she was wanting. But she didn't hide the gleam in her eyes quickly enough.

"I'll show you," said Alex. Slowly, tantalizingly, he drew a coin from his sporran and held it up. It gleamed silver, and Kelpie stared at it greedily. "See?" Alex chuckled and spun it toward her.

Quick as the flash of bright metal in the air, her brown hand shot out to catch it in flight—then dropped, and the coin fell noiselessly on the path. Kelpie sat staring first at it and then at her own shoulder with dismay that was, for a change, perfectly genuine.

"I—I *am* hurt!" she said with astonishment and then hastily snatched up the coin with her good left hand before they should change their minds.

"Not too hurt to be picking up the silver," observed Alex, but the gibe lacked his earlier light tone. Ian had already dismounted and was touching rather gingerly the filthy rags covering the shoulder in question. The lass frankly stank.

This time Kelpie's face showed an honest flicker of pain. "I think it will be sprained, or perhaps out of place," Ian decided and looked at Alex.

Alex looked back at him. "Well, so. And where does she live, then? Where are her people? Perhaps Lachlan could be taking her home."

Ian shrugged. "I think I've seen her with Old Mina and

Black Bogle. Is that so?" he asked Kelpie, who nodded.

Alex raised his eyebrows, not in the least surprised. It was logical that she should belong to the nastiest witch in Scotland.

"Will they be coming along, then?" Ian inquired, and again Kelpie nodded, so bewildered by her unexpected hurt and the pain that was now shooting sharply through her shoulder that she couldn't really think clearly at all.

A glum silence settled on them, broken only by furtive and disapproving mutters from Lachlan. His duty was to be protecting his young masters, and now here they were consorting with witches, and he not able to prevent them at all, at all. He crossed himself.

Ian sighed with relief when the bent figures of Mina and Bogle appeared up the loch-side. They would take care of their lass, and he and Alex could be away home.

But it wasn't that easy. Mina, after taking in the situation at a glance, burst into lamentations and curses that caused the ruddy Lachlan to go pale. "And is it our poor lass you have harmed, wicked beasts that you are?" she wailed, while Bogle stood like a massive old tree in disconcerting silence. "Ocho, ocho, whatever shall we be doing now? May the Evil Eye fall on all your cattle, and the pox upon yourselves, *uruisgean* that you are!"

Ian himself recoiled, not from the curses, but from the evil that was in this horrible old woman. What a dreadful thing that a young lass should belong to such as these! It

was wicked! And yet, what could he do? What could anyone do? Unhappily he stood and stroked his horse's nose
while Alex handled the matter.

Alex did handle it beautifully, with just the right mixture of indulgence, severity, and money. " 'Twas no fault
of ours that she fell, but altogether her own," he told
them. "Still, we are kind-hearted and willing to give you
a bit of silver." And when Mina would have demanded
more, he fixed her with a stern hazel stare that caused her
own pale, muddy eyes to waver and fall. It was all settled
then, and Ian, feeling depressed, turned to mount his
horse.

And then Black Bogle, perhaps feeling that they had
been worsted in the bargaining, reached down and jerked
Kelpie roughly to her feet by the injured arm.

The bit of brutality wrenched a choked cry of anguish
from the girl. Ian whirled around, and Alex was off his
horse in a flying leap and seized Bogle's arm in a grip that
had no gentleness whatever.

"Let go of her, you vile bully!" Alex snarled, red with
fury, while Ian removed the sagging Kelpie from Bogle's
grasp. Lachlan, brandishing a steel dirk a foot long, loomed
ominously behind. . . .

When Kelpie was again able to take an active interest
in events, she heard several voices: a cold, contemptuous
one and a dangerously quiet one, Bogle's growl and Mina's
whine, with dour grumblings in the background. More

money changed hands, and then Mina bent over Kelpie, a cunning, complacent look on her face.

"The fine gentlemen will be taking you home with them to fix your hurt, and we will come to fetch you in the morning," she said. "You will be properly grateful—and behave as I'd be wishing you to," she added meaningly, and Kelpie nodded. She knew quite well what Mina meant —steal whatever she could lay hands on.

Then Ian's concerned face was close to hers as he removed the grimy once-red sash from about her waist and gently bound the injured arm to her side. "And who's knowing what further damage the brute will have done?" he muttered.

After that she found herself lifted to the fearful height of Alex's horse and felt his hard young arm firmly around her. And at a slow walk they set along toward the fork in the path that led through the hills to Glenfern.

By the time they reached the top of the pass, Kelpie was feeling much better. She began to relish the adventure, and she stared with interest at the scene before her as they paused. Ian's face was alight with joy, and Lachlan actually had tears in his eyes. A strange thing that was, she thought wonderingly, ignorant as she was of the love of the Highlander for his own hills. Kelpie knew no home but the ground she walked on.

The glen ran westward ahead of them, a long little valley cradled in hills that were just turning jewel-green with new bracken and showing dark with juniper and white here and there with birch trunks and unmelted snow. On the northern slope stood a weathered gray house which seemed large and grand indeed to Kelpie, and scattered along the glen were little rye-thatched sheiling huts of unmortared stone, nestled into the hillside as if they had grown there. Farther down the glen was a wee loch of silver and blue, ringed with white birches and dotted with green islets.

"Loch nan Eilean—Lake of the Islands," murmured Ian with his heart in his voice, and they rode on down the hill and along to the stables.

Alex lifted Kelpie down from the horse, looked at her oddly, and then with a grin forced open her left hand.

"You little devil!" He laughed. "You've picked my pocket!"

3. Glenfern

KELPIE perched gingerly on a fine brocaded chair near the door of the drawing room and gazed curiously at the scene before her. For house and glen had, on their arrival, erupted into a perfect frenzy of excitement, questions, tears, laughter, shouting, teasing, and hugging.

Dhé! And was this the way most families were behaving toward one another? Kelpie found it baffling and achingly strange, and vaguely annoying; and on the whole she was glad enough to have been forgotten for the moment while she recovered her usual cool head.

Talk rose and surged in a mixture of Gaelic and English. Cameron of Glenfern paced back and forth, the rusty-red and green of his kilt swinging about strong knees. Lady Glenfern, smiling and anxious at once, sat in a carved oak chair, her harebell-blue skirts billowing about her feet. Two small kilted lads pranced with excitement, a bittie lass clamored to be away up in Ian's arms, and a bonnie lass in green, perhaps near Kelpie's age, clung affectionately to both Ian and Alex at once.

Through the open window Kelpie could see Lachlan standing in a ring of laughing and chattering clansmen, and it began to dawn on her that this was no ordinary homecoming. The lads had been away to school in a far-off place in England and had returned quite unexpectedly with important news.

"We knew that King Charles had fled London and set up his court at Oxford," said Glenfern. "And you wrote that Montrose was there, awaiting permission to come and raise an army in Scotland for the King. Now you say he's coming?"

"Aye so," said Alex cynically, "but a bit late, now that Argyll has got all the Lowlands and some of the Highlands well under the thumb of the cursed Covenant! Were you knowing that the Covenant army has crossed the border into England and will be fighting along with the Parliament army against the King?"

"*Dhé!*" exclaimed Glenfern in dismay. "Is it too late, then? Why was the King waiting so long?"

Alex shrugged. "Och, King Charles has a grand talent for not seeing what he doesn't like, and for doing the wrong thing altogether or the right thing too late."

Ian, whose loyalty was a simple and wholehearted thing, frowned at his foster brother. "He's our king and

a Stewart," he reminded him and then turned to his father.
"At any rate, we were thinking we'd best come home while
we still could—and perhaps join Montrose when he
arrives."

None of this meant a great deal to Kelpie, so she began
looking around with greedy wonder at the drawing room.
Och, the glowing fine old silver on the sideboard, the
great portraits on the tapestry-hung walls, the grand,
massive carved furniture worn smooth as silk by time and
polish, and the damask draperies at real glass windows!
It wasn't fair that some people should have so much! They
should be sharing it, they should, and it was up to Kelpie,
she felt, to see to the sharing.

A small silver snuff box was lying on a table near her;
an instant later, it wasn't. Kelpie's long slanted eyes
flickered with satisfaction, but before she could so much
as thrust her loot under her rags, a redheaded figure bent
over her and a sinewy long hand grasped her wrist gently
but with great strength.

"Really, Ian," observed Alex lazily, "you must be paying
more attention to your guest."

"Sssss!" said Kelpie, again wishing she could cast the
Evil Eye on him. But instead the eyes of the entire family
were now on her.

"My sorrow!" said Ian ruefully. "I was forgetting!"

"A shame to all of us, and she injured!" declared his
mother, standing up. " 'Tis only for the night, you were

saying, Ian? Well, so, we will see to the shoulder—but not in the house, I think," she added, looking at Kelpie's filthy clothes.

"No," agreed her husband. "Come away out to the wee room in the stable, which will do nicely, I think."

And Kelpie, who had expected to be beaten and turned out for her theft, stared. They were daft, all of them! But presently she forgot their daftness because of the surprisingly painful business of having her shoulder tended. She gritted her teeth and cursed vigorously, and after it was over she was glad enough to lie down on the small cot in the stable-room and be left alone to sleep.

Kelpie awoke with an oppressive sense of being trapped. Blindly hostile walls and ceiling surrounded her, shutting out sky and wind. In sudden panic she would have leaped up and fled to the safety of outside, but the first movement brought the sharp, forgotten pain of her shoulder. She gasped slightly, blinked, and noticed a pair of dark eyes regarding her from a flower face. It was the wee bit of a lassie she had seen in the big house, who stood watching Kelpie with grave sympathy. She was a tiny thing, her body slight as it rose from the primrose bulk of her long skirts, but Kelpie was disconcerted. The gaze seemed to understand too much.

"Poor lady!" said the mite, shaking her honey-brown head sorrowfully. "Is it a sore bad hurt, then?"

Kelpie said nothing.

Light danced into the dark eyes. "Wee Mairi will kiss it and make it well." Quite undeterred by thoughts of cleanliness, the child leaned over the cot and dropped a soft kiss on the bandages covering Kelpie's shoulder, and then another on her cheek. "Now it will stop hurting, just, and you can be happy," she announced. Crooking a small finger in the old gesture of calling down a blessing from heaven, she turned and trotted out, leaving a shaken Kelpie behind her.

Nothing like this had ever happened to her before! Children had always clung to their mothers, frightened of the witch's lass. No one at all had ever kissed her and Kelpie, to her dismay, found that her eyes had filled with tears. Och, this would never do at all! She must be hard and strong, or else how would she ever survive in the world she knew? She closed her treacherous eyes and concentrated on subduing the weakness.

The weakness was just about subdued when she became aware of more company in the room. This time it was a pair of seven or eight-year-old lads with penetrating blue eyes set in identical tanned faces which were alight with passionate curiosity.

Kelpie, still shaken and very much on the defensive from her encounter with Wee Mairi, glared at them with frank hostility. They went on staring at her with unwavering interest. *Dhé!* They were nearly as disconcerting as

Wee Mairi—and there were two of them. Kelpie decided to take the offensive.

"Ssssss!" she hissed, baring her teeth and beetling her thick eyebrows menacingly. The bright eyes rounded slightly, but with increased curiosity rather than alarm.

"Were you crying?" asked one boy candidly.

"Are you a witch?" demanded the other.

Kelpie considered. It wasn't in the least safe to be thought a witch. It could lead to all sorts of uncomfortable and fatal things. On the other hand, she had never known real safety in any case, and it would be pleasant to impress, or even frighten, these complacent lads.

"I am so," she said with an intimidating scowl. "I can put curses on ye, or the Evil Eye whatever."

They were unintimidated. "Show us!" suggested one hopefully.

"Alex was saying you cannot," challenged the other.

"Och, just you wait!" said Kelpie darkly. "I will be fixing that Alex as ever was!"

"What will you do to him?" persisted the skeptic with morbid curiosity.

"What is your name?" asked his twin.

"Kelpie!" said she in triumph, and at last she had impressed them. For every Highland child knew that a Kelpie was a kind of fairy person, a water witch who wails at night by lochs and rivers for a victim, or cries for admittance at shuttered windows.

"I don't believe it," said the skeptical twin, but he said it halfheartedly.

"Ronald! Donald!" The green-frocked lass who was Kelpie's age stood in the doorway, with a big-boned young woman behind her carrying a tray. "Och, naughty lads! Ye shouldn't be bothering in here, and well ye know it!"

"She's a witch, and a kelpie too," reported one of them, unabashed.

"At least she says so, but we haven't seen her put a spell yet," added the other. "When will you be showing us one?"

The young woman nearly dropped her tray as she hastily tried to make the sign of the cross. Her young mistress looked faintly alarmed but stood her ground. "Be away, now," she told the twins. "I'll take that, Fiona." She took the tray from the quaking Fiona and set it on a stool beside Kelpie's cot.

"We thought you'd be waking up hungry," she said and then looked at Kelpie apologetically, as if ashamed of her own good fortune and pretty clothes. "My name is Eithne," she added, pronouncing it "Ay-na," with the Highland lilt in her voice. "And the twins must not be saying such things—about your being a witch, I mean. Are you?" she asked, overcome by curiosity.

Kelpie already had hand and mouth full of cold venison

pie and new-baked bannocks and had no intention of risking the rest of the food. She shook her head firmly and put on her most innocent and helpless expression.

"Och, no!" she mumbled truthfully around her bannock. "Not I!"

At this moment a gaunt black cat sidled through the open door, spat at Fiona, and with a joyful yowl leaped right on top of Kelpie. This was unfortunate, since black cats were known to have a fondness for witches.

Fiona backed up to the door, crossing herself furiously, and Eithne looked awed. "*Dhé!*" she whispered. "Dubh has never done that before for anyone!"

Kelpie looked at Dubh with a mixture of pleasure and irritation. She liked cats, but this one had timed his appearance poorly.

Dubh looked back at her, great topaz eyes glowing into hers steadily and inscrutably, and his purring filled the room.

"He is wanting some food," suggested Kelpie lamely. But Dubh didn't show the slightest interest in her meal. Instead, he arranged himself comfortably on top of her legs.

"Animals are always liking me," Kelpie went on with better success. Eithne's face brightened and cleared. Of course! And if animals liked a person, it was a sure sign that the person was to be trusted. Eithne, like her brother, wanted to think the best of everyone, especially of those whom life seemed to have treated unfairly. Besides, Kelpie interested her.

Presently she was seated on the edge of the cot, listening to the lurid tale of Kelpie's life and even being shown some of the scars and bruises on the thin shoulders and back. Eithne was hot and shaking with shocked indignation. It was perfectly dreadful, appalling!

And Kelpie, rising to great tragic heights, played up to the most sympathetic audience she had ever had. The long ringed eyes fixed on Eithne's brown ones were soft and luminous and oh, so innocent.

But the "innocent" eyes reminded Alex of Dubh's, as he entered the room and got a good view of both pairs. He hadn't been easy in his mind about Eithne's being in here so long. Ringed eyes like that weren't canny. The lass might well be a witch, at that, though likely too young to be very dangerous. All the same, his foster sister must be protected.

"Come away from her and out of here!" he ordered Eithne brusquely.

He should have known better. She whirled on him, round chin jutting out indignantly. "And will you be judging her unfairly, like all the villagers and all?" Eithne demanded. "Don't deny it, Alex MacDonald! You're thinking hard, suspicious things about her this very minute!"

Alex's sunburned face looked disconcerted at this sud-

den attack, but only for an instant. "Oh, aye," he agreed
cheerfully. "I am that. And why wouldn't I be, with the
many reasons she's given me already? Has she put a spell
on you, *m'eudail?* Best be away to the house and see if
Catriona can break it."

Eithne stamped her foot, but it wasn't easy to find a
retort. "You—you talk like a Covenanter!" she finally
flung at him scathingly and flounced out in a swirl of
petticoats, Fiona behind her.

Alex scratched his red head, more confounded by her
passion than by her rather shaky logic. He grinned wryly
at Kelpie, who looked back at him in triumph.

"Poor innocent waif!" he jeered, putting one foot up on
the edge of the cot, where Dubh spat at it. He rested an
elbow on his kilted knee and stared at Kelpie with interest.
She stared back through slitted eyes.

"Before you're up and away again," he said, casually,
"I've a wee word to be saying to you, and it is this. Unlike Ian and Eithne, I've a nasty suspicious mind, I have."
He wagged his head sadly. "And I've a picture in my head
of you away off tomorrow bearing every movable thing in
the glen hid in your rags, and we sitting here without so
much as a stick of furniture left to us."

"Indeed, and I would never be doing such a thing!"
cried Kelpie indignantly. "How could I be carrying it
all?"

Alex laughed outright. Kelpie scowled. She had been

cursed and beaten often enough, but she had never before been laughed at, and she didn't like it.

Alex stopped laughing and grinned at her. "Well, so, and I've a soft heart in me, so I'll be doing nothing about such matters as pocket-picking or a certain snuff box, nor will anyone else, I think. But"—and he leaned forward a little—"should anything else just happen to be missing when you leave, then you'll be finding the hand of every Cameron and MacDonald, all through the Great Glen and Lochaber from Loch Leven to Loch Ness, turned against you."

Kelpie showed sharp white teeth in a defiant laugh. "Are you thinking I've never heard threats before?"

"Aye, I'm sure you have, and most unpleasant ones," retorted Alex. "But have you ever had one like this carried out, and two entire clans arrayed against you, and every *ghillie* on the watch?"

Kelpie narrowed her eyes. He had her, just! And to have the Great Glen and Lochaber closed against them would be a sore handicap indeed.

"Sssss!" said Kelpie with deep sincerity.

Alex grinned again. "I'm not done," he said briskly. "It seems that my foster sister has given you her friendship. You're not deserving it, of course, but for Eithne that's good enough reason for giving it. Now, I am fond of Eithne, and if you should be taking advantage of her or hurting her in any way, I shall see to it that you are punished—even if I must denounce you as a witch. Do you understand?"

It was a fearful threat, and Kelpie, used to bluster and invective, was unnerved by his very calm.

"*Nathrach!*" She spat. "Remember, witches can curse! Shall I be putting the Evil Eye on you?" And she widened her slanted eyes until the dark and light rings were smoldering circles.

Alex laughed again, infuriatingly. "And if you haven't already put the Evil Eye on me at least three times today, it must be that you have not got it at all. For you've wanted to, haven't you? No, I'll wager you cannot do it."

"Mina can," muttered Kelpie sulkily.

"Now that I'll believe," he agreed readily. "But even the Evil Eye wouldn't save the two of you from being burned as witches, would it?"

Och, and he was so sure of himself! Kelpie saw suddenly that great cunning and apparent submission were her best weapons. "And if I am keeping the bargain?" she hinted, looking at his pocket.

"We've no bargain." Alex corrected her mildly. "I'm no such fool. It's just that I've been telling you in a friendly way what will happen if you should be stealing anything or hurting Eithne, that's all." And he sauntered out, his kilt swinging jauntily about his brown knees.

4. The Daft Folk

KELPIE slept heavily for the first part of the night and then awoke to stare restlessly into the stifling, closed-in darkness. How could a body tell the hour, shut in like this? She must be out into the free air and waiting when Mina and Bogle came for her.

She got up and groped her way out into the warm, horse-scented main part of the stable. Dubh, a blacker shape in the dark, came and wove himself around her ankles as she felt for the door with her good left hand; her right shoulder was still too sore to move.

And then she was outside in the cold sweet air of pre-dawn. The hills to the southeast stood black against a thin ghost of gray in the sky, and the glen was filled with a toneless purple except for the ropes of pearly mist strung down the clefts of the hills and over the loch. A tiny burn and waterfall danced in a white thread at the far end of the glen, and the wind smelled of the sea.

Kelpie drew in her breath deeply, and the beauty of it made a sore ache inside her and a daft desire to cry. It was something deep within her, just, that had these strange feelings now and then, and she must be careful never to let them out.

It was these daft folk at Glenfern who were making her feel peculiar. She must be away from them, away from the trapping walls and alien people, to the freedom of the hills and sky. She slipped like a wraith around to the back of the stable, where the ground sloped upward, wrapping her bare ankles in the wetness of rank grass and heather and stinging nettles, which she had long ago stopped noticing. And at the upper corner a long skinny arm reached out with the swiftness of a snake, seized Kelpie's wrist (fortunately, the uninjured one), and shook her.

"We've been waiting for you this long while!" Mina began pulling her up the hill.

Kelpie came willingly enough. She was almost glad to see Mina's evil old face. She knew where she was with Mina. She could hate and be hated single-mindedly, and always know how Mina would behave. The people at Glenfern were unpredictable and confusing.

Black Bogle was waiting in a clump of snowy-trunked birches halfway up the hill. He said nothing, just grinned without warmth or welcome.

"Well, and what have you got?" demanded Mina, turning upon Kelpie with greedy fingers held out.

"Nothing at all," muttered Kelpie defensively. "The red-haired *uruisg* took back the silver and the snuff box and said if I was taking anything else he would be setting all the Camerons and MacDonalds against us."

Mina cursed Alex and Kelpie both, but with her mind so clearly upon other matters that Kelpie didn't feel the curses would be very effective. "Well, so!" concluded the old woman suddenly. "And just as well, perhaps. For we are wanting you to bide here for a time."

Kelpie stared, her mouth drooping open. *Dhé!* Now Mina was being as unpredictable as anyone in the glen below! "And whatever for, if I cannot be stealing anything?" she demanded. "And why would they be letting me stay?"

Mina struck at her. Kelpie ducked automatically, and Bogle chuckled. He would also have chuckled had the blow landed.

"You'll be persuading them, just," commanded Mina. "Play upon their sympathy. Let them be making you a maidservant if they will—and mind that you be a good one. 'Tis a spy you'll be, to watch and listen, for the lads are fresh from England and knowing about affairs. Be learning how they feel about the King and Mac Cailein Mor and the Lord Graham of Montrose. And keep them feeling kindly toward you, for we may use them one day."

Kelpie hooded her eyes thoughtfully. She had already learned a good bit—but why tell Mina now? Better to wait and see where her own advantage lay and learn what Mina was up to.

"And where will ye be going?" she ventured to ask.

"Never you mind!" snapped Mina. "We will be returning for you when we are ready, and then it may be that you can learn some of the witchcraft you are wanting so badly." Beneath their wrinkled lids her faded old eyes gleamed at Kelpie watchfully.

Kelpie kept her own eyes veiled. She knew how much Mina's promise was worth, but here was hope that Mina might really be going to teach her at last, for her own profit. Kelpie must be very docile, then, and never let Mina suspect what was in her mind.

"Very well so," she agreed indifferently, it being best to show neither reluctance nor enthusiasm.

"Once more with the crystal, then," ordered Mina, producing it; and Kelpie obediently sat down in the dew-heavy clumps of long grass. Her face was lowered meekly, to conceal the knowledge that Mina depended on her to see the picture. The gray light was now growing rosy over the bare top of Meall Dubh. The rosiness was reflected in the shining ball and then moved and scattered.

"A battle!" whispered Kelpie, her eyes large and fixed on the scene. But it wasn't like the other battles she had seen in the crystal—no cavalry charge of armored men on green slopes, but a charge of Highlanders on the steeper, wilder hills of Scotland. She could clearly make out the bright tartans, and the double-handed claymores flashing, and she could almost hear the wailing skirl of the pipes. There was a red-bearded giant in the thick of it, and a slight brown-haired man on a horse, wearing a blue bonnet, and it was he who seemed to be the power behind the charge—though Kelpie couldn't say how she knew. And now the others were fleeing in the fury of the attack, and it seemed to Kelpie that she saw the blue and green Campbell tartan among the defeated.

Her voice muted and hurried, Kelpie described the scene to Mina, leaving out the name of the tartan and any other details that she guessed Mina might not be able to make out for herself.

And now there was a different scene, and there was the brown-haired man, dressed quite unfittingly as a groom, clasping the hand of the red-bearded one, who was looking altogether astonished and overjoyed, and behind them, on the hillside, was a cheering crowd of Highlanders.

"Well?" demanded Mina.

Kelpie shook her head. "A hillside and a crowd of people," she murmured, "but 'tis all cloudy." And then she held her breath.

But Mina didn't seem to know that Kelpie was deceiving her. "I wanted news of Argyll," she grumbled and put the crystal away. Then, after a parting cuff, she strode up the hill with Bogle—and not so much as a parting glance from either of them. Och, they had some pressing purpose, the two of them, and whatever could it be?

The eastern sky was apricot now. The sun would be up in a few minutes, and already golden light was pouring across the very tops of the hills on the far side of the glen, but a fitful wind was coming from the west, promising to bring rain clouds over those same bright hills . . .

What if, after all, Glenfern refused to let her stay? Feeling excited and forlorn at once, Kelpie turned her back on the sunrise and walked slowly down the hill.

She approached the house on lagging feet, suddenly nervous. Ian's father was outside the door, talking to Lachlan and an old man. Lachlan already disliked her, and Glenfern looked as if he could be stern indeed. Kelpie drooped her mouth into an expression of wistful apology, arranged the sling on her arm so that it showed up well, and hovered tentatively a few feet away.

Glenfern's face was kindly enough when he looked up and saw her. "Good morning," he greeted her. "And how are you feeling?"

"Good morning," replied Kelpie, "and well enough,"— making it sound like a brave lie. "But—" She stopped, looking frightened. "Mina and Bogle came," she began, and paused.

"Oh. And you'll be wanting a bit of breakfast before

you're away off with them?" suggested Glenfern with a smile.

"They're away off without me," blurted Kelpie, looking helpless. "They're not wanting me any more."

"*Dhé!*" said Glenfern. He didn't seem overjoyed.

"I have nowhere to go," added Kelpie pathetically, in case he hadn't got the point.

"Aye," said Glenfern, who had got it very quickly. "Well, come away in, and we'll see my wife."

"*Mise-an-dhui!*" said Lady Glenfern when they told her. She looked even less delighted than her husband.

Eithne looked up from sorting and polishing silver. "Och, what a wicked thing!" she exclaimed, her creamy oval face troubled and sympathetic. "And have you no other relations?"

Kelpie shook her head. Wee Mairi, gathering that something was wrong, ran over and slipped her warm little hand into Kelpie's, and the twins looked up in surprise, for they had thought everyone had more relations than could be counted.

"Perhaps she had better be staying with us," they suggested through mouthfuls of buttered scone—an extra breakfast, no doubt. "She could put the Evil Eye on all our enemies, whatever," added Ronald hopefully.

"You're not really a witch, are you?" asked Lady Glenfern seriously. A white witch, of course, was a great benefit to have around, since all her powers were used for good; and the Kirk of the Lowlands had not yet reached far enough into the Highlands to make even white powers dangerous. Still, the lass of Old Mina was more likely to be a black witch, than a white one.

"No!" Said Kelpie vehemently, and with perfect truth. (How she wished she were!) "And I would never be wanting to harm anyone," she added, less truthfully.

Alex, sitting cross-legged on the far window seat, sent her a bright hazel glance of derision, which Kelpie ignored.

Glenfern raised an eyebrow at his wife, sighed, and smiled kindly. "Would you be wanting to stay with us, lassie?" he asked.

"I would so," replied Kelpie forthrightly. This was easier than she had hoped—if only Alex didn't spoil it. "I could be working," she offered meekly. " 'Tis little enough I am knowing about the insides of houses, but I learn quickly."

Alex muffled a snort of laughter. They all glanced at him, but he merely gave Kelpie a look that was both warning and mirthful.

Kelpie, who would have made a good general, seized the offensive boldly. "He is thinking I want to steal things," she announced, nodding her tangled black head in Alex's direction.

"And do you not?" asked Glenfern bluntly.

"Of course," admitted Kelpie candidly. Didn't every-

one? "But I would not be doing it," she went on, her blue-
ringed eyes fixed on Glenfern's, "because you would be
sending me away if I did."

It was the best thing she could have said. Glenfern
lifted his dark head with a shout of delighted laughter.
Everyone seemed pleased and amused, and Kelpie made
a mental note that truth was sometimes even more effective
than a lie. She looked demure and managed at the same
time to shoot a triumphant glance at Alex. But, disap-
pointingly, he only grinned.

"Very well so," decided Lady Glenfern, smiling at her.
"It is not many people can claim to having a friendly
Kelpie staying with them. And I think you have it in you
to be a good lass, and trustworthy."

Kelpie looked at her, deeply shocked. How could a
great lady like this be so foolishly trusting? And all of
them seemed the same—excepting Alex, of course, who
was sensibly suspicious. Kelpie definitely approved of
this, although she hated his uncanny astuteness and his
mockery. As for the rest of them, indeed and indeed, it was
a wonder they had managed to survive so long. Fooling
them was almost too easy, like catching a baby hare with
a broken leg.

She felt the same way all over again on that very afternoon, after a most difficult morning.

The difficulties had begun almost immediately after
Kelpie's too easy acceptance into the life of Glenfern. It

seemed that Lady Glenfern had peculiar ideas on the subject of cleanliness and propriety. To begin with, there was the bath, the first Kelpie had ever had, supervised by the mistress herself, and executed by Fiona and her formidable mother Catriona. Catriona grumbled constantly, and Fiona crossed herself every time Kelpie looked at her—which she did frequently and maliciously.

Then there was the matter of her name. "Have you not a proper Christian name?" asked Lady Glenfern while Kelpie's matted hair was being violently combed and plaited into two long, thick tails. Kelpie, unable to shake her head, and with eyes smarting from the pulling, made a sound that meant no.

"My sorrow!" remarked her new mistress. "A strange thing to be naming a lass for a water witch! Would you not rather be called something else? Rena, perhaps, or Morag?"

But Kelpie caught a glimpse of herself just then in the small mirror that stood on a table, and a fleeting shaft of panic shot through her. It wasn't herself at all! Her face was a stranger, with the dirt off and the hair pulled back wetly to show all of her eyes and forehead and even her fawn-shaped ears. *Dhé!* If they changed her name as well, perhaps she would cease altogether to be herself and become someone else entirely!

"No!" she said vehemently. And the subject was dropped.

But when they gave her a fine-woven blue woolen dress of Eithne's for her very own, and even something to wear under it, she began to take a more favorable view of the situation. And when, in the afternoon, she met Ian coming in the front door, he hardly seemed to know her at first. His eyes opened wide as he shook the heavy rain from his plaidie, and then he gave her one of his rare and sudden smiles that was like sunlight out of the drenching sky. Kelpie grinned back, preening herself frankly in her new finery.

"Och, aren't you grand, just!" Ian said admiringly.

"Oh, aye," agreed Kelpie, seeing no reason to deny it. "But I should have a pocket and a wee bit of silver to put in it," she added hopefully.

Ian laughed at her cheekiness. "Perhaps some day," he said. "But I know that you will not be stealing them, for you have said you won't, and I trust you."

There it was again! Kelpie shook her head in wonder. That wasn't at all the reason she wouldn't be stealing, and how could he be so daft as to think it? His warm brown eyes and the lovely chiseled, sensitive curve of his mouth quite melted Kelpie, and before she could stop herself she was warning him.

"Och," she blurted. "You mustn't be trusting people so easily! It is not safe whatever!"

"Mustn't I trust you, then?" asked Ian gently. "Are you not wanting to be trusted, Kelpie?"

"Indeed so," explained Kelpie kindly. "Everyone is wanting to be trusted, because then it is much easier to fool the ones who trust them. And you may be trusting me because you have a stick over me, but it is foolish to do so otherwise."

They looked at each other pityingly.

"Perhaps people are not so good as I would like to think," said Ian slowly. "But I think they are not so bad as you have found them, either, Kelpie. And I would liefer trust mistakenly than to mistrust unfairly. Do you understand that?"

"No," said Kelpie.

5. Bewitchery

IT WAS a strange new life she was in, indeed! Walls and roof were like a trap at first, although it was a grand thing to be warm and dry with all the storm demons howling over the earth. It was strange to have certain tasks at certain times, too, and not easy for a gypsy lass to whom time was nothing. It was strange to eat hot meals three times a day, and at a table, with the heat coming from the huge kitchen fireplace. But it was not so strange to have the servants lowering at her suspiciously. For the clanspeople of the glen, unlike their chief and his family, never trusted this water witch for a moment. An evil sprite she was, and no mistake about it. They watched every move she made.

Still, suspicion was less after her first Sunday there, after she had gathered with the others to hear Glenfern read the service. It was well known that no witch would dare enter a church or hear the Holy Word, lest the roof fall in or some other dire thing happen. Kelpie herself was uneasy about this at first. True, she was not a witch, but she wanted to be, and she had read the crystal with Mina, and she wasn't altogether certain what might happen. Still, it wasn't a proper church, with a priest, but only Glenfern reading the Anglican service—and in any case, she dared not refuse. So she went, heart beating faster than usual, and was greatly relieved when nothing dreadful happened.

True to her promise, Kelpie was diligent and learned quickly. Her reward was free time to wander in the encircling hills or to be with the other young people—and this was strangest of all, for they played and chattered and joked in a way quite novel to Kelpie, with laughter among them, and an ease and affection that held no wariness. Under the bewitchment of it, Kelpie found herself dropping her own guard more and more often. She liked being with them! There was more joy in it than in shouting and dancing alone on a hilltop; a different excitement from that she felt when cutting purses. As the days passed, she often had to remind herself of the advice she had given Ian. To be too relaxed could be dangerous—especially with that sharp-minded Alex about.

Still, she couldn't help enjoying those hours, and presently something clicked in her mind, and she understood the baffling thing they called teasing.

Kelpie, Eithne, Ian, and Alex were sitting nearly waist-deep in the tangle of heather and bog-myrtle that rimmed Loch nan Eilean on a sunny afternoon.

"Are you *sure* you're not wanting a proper name besides 'Kelpie'?" Eithne asked, her soft voice worried and laughing at once. "It seems so insulting, just, that your parents . . ."

Parents? Suddenly Kelpie remembered what Bogle had said. Suppose she had truly been stolen? Suppose she were really the daughter of a chief? Och, the glory of it! Wealth and importance, lovely gowns and jewels, silver buckles on real leather shoes, and a silver belt around her waist, and oh, the safety of never having to run from angry crowds . . .

"*Dhé!*" she announced eagerly. "Mina and Bogle will not be my parents, at all." She paused dramatically and prepared to launch the rest of her news. How startled and respectful they would be! Why hadn't she thought of it sooner?

"Och, now!" Alex turned twin sparks of laughter upon her. "And haven't I been waiting, just, for you to be telling us? Kelpie has suddenly remembered," he explained to the others solemnly, "that she was stolen by the gypsies when a wee bairn and is truly the daughter of a great chief, or perhaps of royal blood."

"How did you know?" began Kelpie and then stopped. The others were chuckling as at a great joke. Alex had put the blight of ridicule on her story—though it was at least half true. And now no one would ever be believing it at all!

"Beast!" she spat. "It is *true!*"

"As ever was!" agreed Alex jauntily and ducked her angry fist. Then he caught her wrist, put it firmly in her lap, and sat grinning at her. "You're a wonderful wee liar, aren't you just?" he observed admiringly.

"Ou, aye," admitted Kelpie a trifle smugly before she realized that he had tricked her again. "But this time," she pointed out with indignation, "I am not lying."

"And would you not be saying the same thing if you were lying?" he persisted.

This time Kelpie saw the trap, but she was already in it. "Of course," she admitted with forthright logic. "For what would be the good of lying if you did not say it was the truth? But"—she bristled, slanted brows scrambling themselves darkly above her short nose—"*this* time it *is* true!"

Alex laughed.

Kelpie tried for at least the twentieth time to put the Evil Eye on him. The result was a poisonous look, if not a blighting one. "Wicked, evil-minded beast!" she told him earnestly.

Ian looked at Alex judiciously. "Och, no; not wicked," he said. "He's a bit evil-minded, 'tis true, and surely daft."

Kelpie blinked.

"Aye, daft enough," agreed Eithne happily. Were you

knowing, Kelpie, that he's altogether foolish about an
English lass, his cousin Cecily in Oxford? And yet all he
can be saying of her is that she is like her own wee kitten,
and that he will marry with her some day."

Alex grinned brazenly. "Well, and with who else?" he
demanded. "You would not be having me, *m'eudail*."

"*Dhé*, no!" agreed Eithne promptly. "I'd as lief marry
the twins!"

"Mayhap Kelpie would have him," suggested Ian lazily,
and then he and Eithne shouted with laughter at the looks
of sheer horror on both faces.

"Mercy!" begged Alex, getting to his knees and clasping
his hands pleadingly. "Anything but that! Curse me all
you wish, water witch, but *please* do not marry me!"

Kelpie looked at him. It was then that something
clicked. "Very well so," she agreed with enthusiasm. "And
what sort of curse would you be wanting?"

She went back to the house a little later, looking thoughtful and with a pleasant feeling in the heart of her—not
merely because, for once, she had got the better of Alex,
but also because of the thing that happened between
people when they teased. It was a warm and happy thing
that turned insults to joking and the hatred of Alex to
something kinder. For surely a body did not tease where
he hated! And surely he had been half teasing her from
the first.

Kelpie's blue eyes glinted happily as she hurried into the big stone-floored kitchen, so that Marsali the cook almost smiled at her and Fiona for once forgot to cross herself.

"And about time it is, too!" Marsali grunted, remembering her doubts about Kelpie. "The mistress has been looking for you while you were playing like a fine lady. Here, now, be helping to pluck this fowl, and let Master Donald go tell her that you're here."

Kelpie glanced at the half of the twins who was arming himself for an afternoon of fishing, with a huge packet of scones and butter. "That's Ronald," she said absently as she picked up the small brown pheasant.

Three pairs of eyes focused on her in sudden sharp attention, for it took far more than a brief glance to tell one twin from the other. In fact, only their mother and Wee Mairi could invariably do it.

"I'm Donald," asserted the twin, his eyes sparkling at her.

"You're Ronald." Kelpie contradicted him serenely, hardly glancing up from her plucking job.

Marsali at once took sides. "Och, now, will you be calling the wee master a liar?" she demanded indignantly, her fists planted against her hips.

"Ou, aye," said Kelpie. "He will be teasing you," she added, pleased to recognize it.

Fiona looked shocked. Marsali peered suspiciously from

Kelpie to the twin, who giggled. "Och, well, then," said Marsali, her ruddy face now ruddier with indignation, though she was not quite sure at whom to direct it. "Fine it is that Master Ronald has the wee mole on the back of his neck." And she strode over to the grinning lad and lifted up the shoulder-length dark hair to look at the neck beneath. Kelpie went on plucking, perfectly sure of herself and feeling rather smug.

"Master Ronald it *is!*" Marsali clucked, and Fiona crossed herself and edged away from Kelpie. "How could you be knowing, save with the Black Power?"

"Aye," demanded Ronald. "How were you knowing, Kelpie? Was it witchcraft?"

Kelpie grinned and shrugged. She couldn't really tell how she knew. It wasn't the look of them, but rather the feel. Donald had a more aggressive and challenging tone, and Ronald more a feel of hungry curiosity. But how could a body explain this kind of knowing? No, they would just have to think it witchcraft.

"*Mise-an-dhui!*" muttered Marsali, regarding her warily. Fiona had backed against the far wall. Donald appeared in search of his twin, and the two went into a conference. Presently they came out of it and presented a solid front to Kelpie, sturdy legs planted wide.

"That is no proof you are a witch," announced Donald. "Mother and Wee Mairi can tell us apart, and they are no witches, only Mother is knowing us too well and Mairi has Second Sight."

Kelpie yielded to temptation, made a horrible grimace, and began weaving mysterious signs in the air with her fingers. Fiona screeched, and Marsali turned pale. The twins stood their ground, grinning, belligerent, deeply interested—and just faintly worried.

"Now whatever is all this?" It was Lady Glenfern herself, her full mauve skirts nearly filling the wide doorway, with Eithne, round-eyed, just behind.

"Witchcraft!" squeaked Fiona.

Kelpie flushed guiltily and found a sudden lump in her throat. Och, here was a mess! Why had she done such a foolish thing? All in fun it was, and yet who would believe her for a minute? Now she would be punished and sent away—and, for once, for a thing of which she was innocent! The novelty of the situation was so shattering that for once she lost her glib tongue. She simply stared at her mistress, her eyes growing wide with frustration and despair.

The twins and Marsali broke into simultaneous explanations—all slightly different—with Fiona putting in exclamation points here and there, so that it was some time before Lady Glenfern could get an idea of what had happened. When she did, she turned questioningly to Kelpie, who was still trying to think up some lie that

sounded more plausible than the truth. But Eithne spoke
first.

"Och, then, Mother!" she said, laughter and distress in
her voice. "She was teasing; I am sure of it. Look you how
the twins are always at her to cast a spell, and Fiona just
begging to be teased by the very look of her. I am sure
that was the way of it! Was it not, Kelpie?"

Kelpie nodded a bit sullenly. This was humiliating.
She wished she really had power to do a wee magic spell
and dared show them, just to see their surprise.

"Well—" Lady Glenfern hesitated, inclined to believe
it, but not quite sure. After all . . .

At that moment Wee Mairi popped into the kitchen,
looking, in her full skirts, like a fairy child caught in an
overblown rose. And, like a fairy child, she knew instantly
that something was wrong, and what to do about it. She
pattered across the floor and slipped her small, soft hand
into Kelpie's.

"This is *my* Kelpie," she announced, smiling angelically
at her mother. " 'Tis myself loves her, and you must not
be cross at her."

"There, Mother!" crowed Eithne. "Wee Mairi loves her,
and Mairi has the Second Sight; you said yourself that
she is never making a mistake about a person!"

Lady Glenfern relaxed. "Aye so," she agreed and smiled
at Kelpie. "I can well see how you were tempted to tease,"
she admitted and then became grave. "But you must be

careful, lass. To joke about such matters could cause you sore trouble."

Kelpie hardly heard the warning. Her hand was gripping the small one still protectively clinging to it, and she found herself again seized by an alarming surge of feeling for its owner. Och, the fair, sweet heart of her . . .

Wee Mairi chose this instant to lean confidingly against Kelpie and peer up with a beguiling smile. "*My* Kelpie," she repeated.

And Kelpie was swallowed in a tide of the first real love she had ever known. She found it extremely upsetting. All her training and experience warned her that it was dangerous to be trapped into this sort of feeling. It left one vulnerable, could lead one into foolishness. And here she was, bewitched, unable to help it! She scowled helplessly.

Lady Glenfern, seeing her distress, mercifully took her from the kitchen for the rest of the day and set her to work at a simple bit of weaving. For an hour or so Kelpie sat alone, brooding. Eithne came in for a while to work at her own more complicated length of Cameron tartan, but Kelpie was so unsociable that she left again.

And then the twins arrived, dark heads cocked to one side, eyes dancing at her impishly. "We have found you," they announced in triumph.

"Fine I know it," growled Kelpie, refusing to look at them.

Undaunted, they seated themselves on two wee creepie-
stools and regarded her with affable curiosity. "There is
a thing that we have in our minds," they told her.

"I am doubting that!" snapped Kelpie.

The twins digested this insult and then chuckled. "I
am liking you fine," said Donald, "even though you are
not a witch."

Kelpie, touched again on that newly sensitive spot, shot
the shuttle through the warp with unnecessary violence
and said nothing.

"Why were you saying you are a witch when you are
not?" asked Ronald with interest. "Why," he continued,
getting warmed up, "do Fiona and the others think you
are? Would you like to be? Are you truly Old Mina's girl?
Is she your Grannie Witchie? If you were a witch, Kelpie,
what would you do first of all?"

"Put a spell of silence on the tongue of you," retorted
Kelpie and found that her ill humor was beginning to
evaporate. It was impossible not to smile back at their
cheeky grins, not to chuckle when they said that Mother
would probably approve such a spell. The atmosphere
became quite congenial.

"I thought you were going fishing," observed Kelpie.

The twins looked depressed. "We were," they agreed.
"But Father is come back from seeing Lochiel and told
us to bide here for our lessons that we missed this morning. I think 'twill take him a wee while to find us in here,

whatever," added Ronald cheerfully, and Kelpie grinned again.

"We are learning about the war between King Charles and Parliament and the Covenant," volunteered Donald sadly, "and we could do fine *not* knowing about it. Grown-ups are gey confusing, so they are, and sometimes I think gey foolish besides, and we are not understanding it all very well."

"Are you loving King Charles?" demanded Ronald.

"Ou, aye," murmured Kelpie vaguely and hastened to turn the question. "Are you?" she countered.

"As ever was!" they chorused instantly. "Is he not our King, and a Stewart, besides?"

Well, Kelpie had already known that Glenfern was pro-Royalist. "And so the King is always right?" she pursued, trying to think what else to ask.

"Och, no!" said the twins in surprise. "No one is always right," they informed her gravely. "Except," they added, "for Father."

Kelpie put her shuttle through the wrong way and had to take it out again, her lip twitching ever so slightly. The twins, having settled that subject of conversation, looked at her hopefully. "Can you," they asked, "tell us a story?"

Now if there was one thing Kelpie could do better than any other, it was to tell stories—pathetic tales to earn sympathy or a copper, outrageous lies to escape impending trouble, embroidered yarns of her own adventures, old

gypsy stories, eerie folk tales of the wee people and other
uncanny beings, or fanciful bits and snatches that she
wove for herself among the hills or beside the campfire.
Her eyes sparkled. "Fine I can that!" she asserted and
dropped her voice to an eerie pitch.

"Have you ever," she whispered, "heard of the *uruisg* of
Glenlyon?"

They shook their heads and drew their stools nearer.

"Well, then." Kelpie paused, shuttle in hand. "It was a
farmer's wife who was making porridge for breakfast on
a wet morning, when who should come walking in but an
uruisg. Och, a slippery, damp, uncouth monster he was,
half man and half goat; and wasn't he just sitting himself
down at the fire to dry, and not so much as a wee greeting
to her? Well, the farmer's wife was fair angered at his
impertinence, and she having to step over and around him
every minute, so presently she just lifted a ladle of the
boiling porridge from the pot over the fire, and poured it
over him, just. Well, at that he leaped up, howling, and
ran out the door and never dared set foot in that house
again. . . ."

When Glenfern finally tracked down his elusive twins
some time later, Kelpie had got very little weaving done,
but she had made a place for herself forever in the hearts
of Ronald and Donald.

6. The Picture in the Loch

"'Tis a terrible complicated matter, the war," objected Eithne doubtfully as she began basting a sleeve into what was to be a fine linen shirt for Ian's birthday. "I fear I'd only be confusing you."

Kelpie surveyed the four or five yards of red and green tartan wool which constituted a kilt for a small lad, and wondered how even Donald could have managed to tear such stout weave. "I could not be more confused than I am," she pointed out, "for I am knowing nothing at all. Tell me at least a little."

Eithne sighed and obeyed. "Well," she began hesitantly, "you know that King Charles is King of England and Scotland both?" Kelpie nodded. "But in both countries are representative bodies of men called Parliaments, and they

help to rule. They are supposed to agree with the things
the King does, and it is the English parliament who must
vote to give him things like extra money when he needs
it—which he usually does."

She paused to squint critically at her basting, and Kelpie waited. Somehow she had developed a great eagerness
to learn about the matters which had thrown England and
Scotland into civil war. "Aye, go on," she murmured.

"Well, so. Neither King Charles nor his father before
him has got along well with Parliament. King and Parliament each said the other will be trying to take more rights
and power than they should have, and they became angry.
Parliament would refuse to vote money for the King, so
the King would dissolve Parliament, which meant that
they could not meet any more to vote on anything at all
until King Charles called them back, and so everyone was
unhappy."

She bit off her thread and held the shirt closer to the
dim light which filtered through the thick diamond-
shaped mullion panes of the casement window. "And
then"—she sighed—"religion came into it. Father," she
remarked severely, "says that religion should never be
mixed with politics, but they do not listen to wise people
like Father, and so there is trouble."

"What has religion to do with it?" asked Kelpie curiously. She had never known anything of religion for herself, only that the stern Kirk of the Lowlands had severe

views on all other faiths, on fun and laughter, and most particularly on witches. But the Anglican services here at Glenfern seemed peaceful and vaguely pleasant, even though she did not understand them.

"Och!" protested Eithne, but Kelpie's face was implacable, so she went on. "Well, the Catholics and Protestants do not like each other, and especially the Protestants of the new Reformed Church, like the Puritans in England and the Calvinist Covenanters in Scotland—and we Anglicans caught in the middle. King Charles is Anglican, but the Parliament is mostly Puritan, I think. At any rate, they were very angry when the King married Queen Henrietta, who is a Roman Catholic and said she would turn the country all Catholic and burn Protestants at the stake. And the Catholics said the Protestants were trying to rule the country and force their religion on everyone, and so it was a fine braw quarrel for years, with religion and politics all mixed together."

Kelpie carefully selected a strand of wool to match the soft, dull red of the Cameron tartan. This was the most difficult bit of mending she had yet been trusted with. "Mmm," she murmured after a minute, turning her mind back to the conversation. "And then?"

It was Eithne's turn to pause, while the rain beat against the casement windows. Wee Mairi turned from her doll to lift a merry smile in the direction of "her Kelpie," who felt a new pang of affection. Och, the bonnie wee thing!

Eithne scowled at the shirt and then glanced up at Kelpie with a rueful shrug. "Ou, I cannot mind me of all the details." She sighed again. "But the quarrel turned into fighting."

"But what of Scotland?" demanded Kelpie. "What had it to do with us at all?"

"Why," interrupted the dry voice of Alex, "King Charles himself must be bringing that on!" They looked up to see him standing in the doorway, a shirt in his hand and a wry grin on his angular face. "Scotland might have been loyal to him, even though all the Lowlands are Calvinist, and even more rigid than the Puritans, but he had the bright idea of forcing the Anglican prayer book on Scotland. And the next thing he knew, there was a Solemn League and Covenant formed against him, and Scotland divided as England was, with Lowlands against the King, and most of the Highlands loyal to him."

Eithne looked both relieved and worried, while Kelpie studied Alex's expression in the dim light, not quite certain if he were teasing or not. She decided not—for once. There was a faint note of bitterness in his voice. "I thought you were a King's man!" she challenged him.

"I am so," he returned promptly and unpropped himself from the doorway. "Look you, Eithne," he went on, crossing the room to her. "I have ripped my shirt sorely and am needing a bonnie sweet lass to mend it for me."

Eithne tilted her chestnut curls at him and wrinkled up

her nose in an impish grin. "If I do," she said, bargaining, "will you be explaining the rest of the war to Kelpie?"

"*Dhé!*" said Alex and raised both eyebrows at Kelpie.

"She is truly wanting to know," said Eithne sternly, "so do not be teasing her, Alex. And I am gey muddled about it, and you knowing so much more, with having been at Oxford and even seeing the King and his family yourself. Will you?"

" 'Tis a hard bargain," complained Alex, "and I am thinking I pity the man who will one day marry you, Eithne *m'eudail.*" He perched on the corner of the massive table, his kilt falling in heavy folds about his lean knees. "Well, then, and what bit of my great knowledge should I be sharing with you first?"

Kelpie gave him a wicked pointed smile. "Tell me," she said softly, "in one word, just, *what are they fighting for?*"

"My sorrow!" exclaimed Alex, straightening up as if he had sat on a thistle. "Is that all?"

"Don't you know?" asked Kelpie tauntingly. "I will tell you, then. They're fighting for power. Is it not so?"

Alex resumed his perch and surveyed her ruefully. "Och, and are you not the young cynic!" he observed. "And you have shocked my foster sister, too." For Eithne was looking both dismayed and indignant. Both girls had forgotten their sewing for the moment and sat staring at Alex challengingly, waiting for his opinion.

He laughed. "I fear me I shall anger you both," he

remarked, "and go through the rest of my life with an evil
spell on my head and a torn sleeve in my shirt."

"Well?" demanded Kelpie.

Alex gave her a crooked grin. "Sorry I am to agree with
you even in part," he confessed, "but no doubt some men
are fighting for power. No, no, Eithne," he added as she
opened her mouth. "Do not deny it too quickly. What
about Argyll?"

Eithne subsided.

"On the other hand, Alex *avic*, there is Montrose." It
was Ian. He pulled up a hassock and ranged himself
quietly but firmly on Eithne's side.

"Montrose?" asked Kelpie.

"Aye," said Ian, turning his warm smile upon her. "James
Graham of Montrose, and he one of the finest, truest men
under the sun. He it is who is named to fight for the King's
cause in Scotland, even to form and organize the army.
And he is fighting for no selfish reason whatever, but only
for what he believes to be right. Alex cannot deny it, for
we both met and talked to him last winter in Oxford."

"Indeed and I'll not deny it," agreed Alex amiably,
"though Kelpie might. My point was just that all men are
not like Montrose, and my proof of it is still Argyll. Och,
and have you done, my sonsie Eithne?" he added as she
held up the mended shirt. "Come away, then, Ian, and
let's be outside. I believe the sun is going to come out."

And they were gone before Kelpie could ask about Argyll. Perhaps it was as well, she decided, going back to her mending. For she really thought she had heard quite as much as she could absorb all in one lump.

Eithne flickered a mischievous sideways glance at her. "And wasn't I warning you 'twas complicated?" she murmured.

As if by tacit agreement, no one brought up matters like war and politics for some time. After all, it was easy enough, in that peaceful, secluded glen, to put such things far out of mind. Kelpie's free hours were full enough, as spring days became longer, with other things. Wee Mairi tagged along with her, a self-appointed guardian, and the glenspeople had learned to hide their hostility when Mairi was there. The twins were insatiably hungry for more stories—and so, for that matter, were the older young people. Books were rare and precious, and mostly devoted to serious and difficult subjects. And, as Ian generously remarked on a sunny afternoon by the loch, Kelpie was a master at telling tales.

Alex grinned impishly. "She is that!" he agreed with a wicked twinkle in his eye and a double meaning to his voice which Kelpie chose to ignore.

"Next time I will tell you about the *sithiche* (fairies) of Loch Maree—*if* you are all very kind to me," she said blandly and glanced impudently at Alex.

She sat on alone by the loch for a little while after the

others had left, thinking about things. How Alex had changed since she first met him! He was much nicer than she had thought. And she had begun to like his teasing and mockery, for it was all good-humored. . . . Or was it perhaps herself had changed? And if so— She rolled over to lie full-length on her face in the fragrant long grasses and pondered. Then, lazily, she stretched until her head was over the edge of the loch.

What was her real self like? Had that changed? Could it?

The bank at this point rose abruptly about two feet above the glassy surface of the water, with tough curling roots of heather overhanging the edge. Kelpie reached down skillfully, scooped up a handful of the cold water, and drank it from her palm before it could run through her fingers. The surface rippled slightly and returned to its mirror stillness, with sky, hills, and trees reflected so clearly that it would be hard to tell the reflection from the real. Or was one, perhaps, as real as the other?

She stared down at her own face, still looking indecently bare with all the thick dark hair pulled back into plaits. Was that any less real—or more—than the scenes she saw in Mina's crystal?

And then it was no longer her own face she was seeing, but a town street and an ugly-tempered crowd surging down it. Not merely annoyed, that crowd, but murderous.

Kelpie shivered a little, for she knew too well how bestial a mob could be. And this one had a victim, for there was savage satisfaction in the grim Lowland faces above their sober Covenanter garments, pressing closer and closer. . . . And there was Ian! Whatever could he be doing in the Lowlands? Pushing through the crowd, he was; and Alex came after, shouting at him, his angular face all twisted with fury. And now they were closer, and Alex was catching up to Ian. . . . Alex was lifting his sword, and through the crowd Kelpie could see him bring it down savagely. . . . *Dhé!* Ian had fallen, his dark head vanished in the throng! And Alex's sword with blood on it!

Kelpie jerked with horror, and a bit of dry heather plopped into the water—and the picture was gone. Nor did it return, though she waited, staring at the still water and brooding bitterly.

Dhé! That serpent Alex! She had never liked him from the beginning! And now he was going to turn on his foster brother, strike him down from behind, perhaps kill him— for the Sight never lied.

She tried to tell herself that it didn't matter to her, but it was too late. Ian had crept into her heart, and Wee Mairi, and the rest of them. Even Alex, deceitful scoundrel that he was, had somehow tricked her into liking him— for a while, anyway. But now she knew better. Och, she must try to warn Ian! Even if he could not prevent it, perhaps he could be on his guard, could put off the evil day of it, could duck in time to save his life.

Dismayed, angry, resolute, Kelpie got to her feet, smoothed down the full folds of her blue dress, and started back up the loch.

Now what, wondered Alex, had got under the skin of their wolf cub lately? For there was a new venom toward himself—and after he had been thinking her nearly tamed, too. Aye, a wolf cub: belligerent, cunning, snarling, biting, thieving, destructive—and yet innocent, as a wolf cub is innocent because it knows nothing else.

But she had been changing. She had been learning trust and affection, even to play and tease. And now, suddenly, there was a new and deadly hatred smoldering at him from those ringed eyes. It was puzzling, it was, and rather less amusing than her old spitting indignation had been; and even though it could hardly be a tragedy to him, still it was disconcerting. Alex kept a wary eye on her, lest she should decide to take her *sgian dhu* to his back.

As for Kelpie, she found the business of warning Ian a bit harder than it had seemed. For one thing, it was none so easy to find him alone, for he and Alex were usually together and about their own affairs, while Kelpie had her tasks in the house. In the evenings the family sat together in the withdrawing room, which was not Kelpie's place. The big warm kitchen, or her wee cot in Marsali's room, was where she belonged, or—more often—away by herself outside, in the pale half-light of the long northern gloaming. For summer was drawing near, and darkness now merely brushed down late upon the world and, like a gull's wing, quickly lifted.

So she glared at Alex and did her tasks and kept her eyes and ears open and bided her time. And at last Alex went off for a few days to visit his brother in Ardochy. And the next evening Kelpie, on one of her rambles, saw Ian on the hill above her, quietly looking down over the glen.

Kelpie drew near, and then paused. Och, a braw lad he was! But how might she be approaching him best? It might be he wanted to be alone. Before she could decide, Ian saw her, smiled, beckoned, his face oddly blurred in the half-light that turned all things gray. She sat beside him and for a minute followed his gaze over the long shadowed cup of the glen, lit by the silver gleam of Loch nan Eilean.

Finally Ian stirred and spoke. "I wish I might never need to leave it again," he said wistfully.

Did he love it so? Kelpie dimly sensed that he did; but she did not understand, for she herself had no roots to her heart, but only a wanderlust to her feet. "And must you, then?" she asked. Why could Ian not be doing as he pleased, since he was the heir to Glenfern?

"Aye so," he said, a bit more briskly. "For I must finish my schooling if I am to be a fit chieftain and leader to my people. However"—he brightened considerably—"I think we'll not be able to return to Oxford for some time, with the war moving northward and becoming more serious, and Argyll endangering all the Highlands."

Now was the moment for her to warn him about Alex. But it was also a chance to ask about Argyll and put off the more difficult thing. "Tell me about Argyll!" she urged.

Ian turned to look at her with friendly interest. "You've a good head on you, haven't you, Kelpie? Mother says you're quick to learn and that you speak English as well as Gaelic. Are you truly interested in national affairs, then?" Kelpie nodded.

"Well, then," began Ian, "you know who Argyll is, do you not? Mac Cailein Mor, Chief of Clan Campbell in the Highlands, and also head of the Covenant Army of the Lowlands. So he has that power added to the power of his own clan, and he uses it ill, Kelpie. He is a vicious man, cruel, ambitious, and vindictive."

Kelpie could not resist a gibe. "And is he not also a Campbell, and his clan at feud with yours?" she remarked.

Ian flushed. Even in the dusk she could see it. " 'Tis not

that!" he protested. "I am not one to hate a man for his name, Kelpie! And in any case, my own uncle married a Campbell lass; and the son of Lochiel, our own clan chief, married Argyll's sister, and we are anxious to be at peace. But Argyll, devil that he is, wishes to dictate his own terms entirely. Do you know what he has done, Kelpie? He has taken his nephew Ewen—Lochiel's own grandson, who will be chief of the Camerons some day—and is keeping him at his own castle of Inverary. He says he wishes to see to his education—and I can guess what kind of education 'twill be—but do you see that Ewen is hostage for Lochiel's actions? And if Lochiel dares to take the side of the King against Argyll—"

"Mmmm," said Kelpie, seeing.

"Nor is it just our clan," Ian went on, deep anger in his voice. "He was commissioned to secure the Highlands for the Covenant, which is bad enough, for we have not tried to inflict our politics or religion on them. But Argyll has used his commission and the Lowland army to settle his private grudges. He burned the great house of Airly, with no enemy there but a helpless woman. And he burned and ravaged the lands of MacDonald of Keppoch, and is even now laying waste the lands of Gordon of Huntly. They say he would make himself King Campbell, and a black day for Scotland if he should."

Kelpie remembered the face she had seen once in the crystal, which Mina had called Mac Cailein Mor, Marquis

of Argyll. A cold, cruel face it had been, with twisted
sneering mouth, a heavy and pendulous nose, and a squint
in the crafty eyes of him, so that one couldn't be just sure
what he was looking at.

"Aye," she agreed suddenly. "He is a red-haired *uruisg*.
I have been seeing him helping with his own hands to
fire the homes and burn people too." She didn't add that
the people burned were accused of witchcraft, as this
might not be a tactful thing to mention.

"You've seen that?" exclaimed Ian.

"In the crystal, only," confessed Kelpie. "I was also seeing him mounting the scaffold to be hanged," she remembered with relish. "But," she added regretfully, "he
was looking much older then."

"*Dhé!*" exclaimed Ian, deeply impressed. "I did not
know you were having the Second Sight, Kelpie."

"Aye," said Kelpie. And here was her opening. "Ian!"
she blurted, quite forgetting to give him a respectful title.
"You must not be trusting Alex MacDonald."

"Not trust Alex?" Ian turned a dumfounded face to
hers. And then he laughed. "Och, Kelpie, there is no one
in the world I trust better! We are sworn brothers, and if
my life were to rest in the two hands of him, there is no
place I would sooner have it."

"And you would lose it, then," said Kelpie flatly. "For
I had a Seeing, and his sword fell upon you from behind,

and you fell. And there was anger on his face and blood upon his sword."

Ian's face was a pale blob in the dusk, and she could not see it turn white—and yet she knew, somehow, that it did. For the Second Sight never lied.

And in spite of that, Ian shook his head. "I cannot believe it, Kelpie," he said quietly. "It is a mistake, for the sun would fall from the sky before Alex could be untrue."

Kelpie thrust an angry face, long eyes glittering, close to his. "You think I am lying, but I am not. I would have been warning you, even though it is of no profit to me, whatever. But it is a spell he has cast upon you! And," she added bitterly, "you will be discovering it too late."

7. The Return of Mina and Bogle

SUMMER was upon the Highlands. The serene curves of the hills glowed with a hundred shades of green and tawny and rose, all with a faintly unreal, spirit-of-opal quality, so that the distances looked no more solid than a rainbow.

Kelpie breathed the salt wind as she climbed higher above the glen, and stared hungrily at the distant hills. For she was beginning to feel restless. A wee glen was not space enough, and there were too many people, too much routine, and she must away to the hills to be alone. Here were only the mild shaggy cattle peering mournfully from behind long fringes of hair, and the hares and red deer, the hill larks and whaups and gulls, and an eagle—high and alone in the free air.

Her acute senses had been lulled by the months of security at Glenfern, and she was startled to see the bent, wiry figure of Mina rise unexpectedly from behind a clump of juniper.

They looked at each other, and Kelpie's expression could not possibly have been mistaken for delight. Mina took one good look at it, swung back her strong, scrawny arm, and aimed it at Kelpie.

It seemed that Kelpie's reactions as well as her senses had become rusty. She didn't duck in time. And, since Mina had fully expected her to, the resounding smack startled and pained them both.

Mina shook her stinging hand and glared at Kelpie as if the girl had done it on purpose. Kelpie, her head ringing, glared back. And Black Bogle, who had appeared as silently as his eerie namesake, shook with malicious laughter.

"*Amadain!*" grumbled Mina sourly. "Forgotten everything you ever knew! Fine-lady clothes and clean face, and hands that will have lost all their cunning—such as it was. Blind and deaf and slow as a sleeping snail. *Amadain!*"

"Sssss!" remarked Kelpie, looking and sounding like a wrathful snake. She had forgotten how ugly and mean and dirty Mina was. Och, how she hated her!

Mina looked pleased. She enjoyed Kelpie's impotent hatred. And Kelpie, knowing this, controlled her feelings and hooded her eyes and made her sharp-jawed small mouth curl upward. She had been a fool to show her feelings at all at all!

"Come away, then," ordered Mina, suddenly becoming brisk. "You have kept us waiting long enough! Why weren't you coming as soon as you got my message?"

"What message?" asked Kelpie blankly. Mina's eyes blazed with fury and humiliation. Bogle laughed aloud, and Kelpie knew that Mina had tried to send her a message by magic—and it hadn't worked. Och, but she must say something quickly, or no telling what Mina might do!

"It would be yon red-haired serpent down there," she said improvising hastily. "He was no doubt setting up a spell to prevent your message from reaching me. Teach me to say spells, Mina," she wheedled, "so that I may set one on him."

It worked. Mina's pride was saved, and her wrath turned from Kelpie to Alex. "I will be cursing him myself," she growled. "He is the same one who would not pay me enough when you were hurt, and who would not let you steal? Very well so! He will pay, and the others as well. We will go now and demand your wages before you leave."

Leave? Kelpie's heart sank. Back to the old life of fear, hatred, beatings? Away from Wee Mairi and Ian and the companionship and teasing? She backed up a step and braced herself.

"What for should I want to leave?" She stuck out her jaw rebelliously, and Mina slapped it.

"Because I am saying so!" she snarled. "And because I will put an evil curse on you if you do not obey."

Kelpie prudently pulled in her smarting jaw and considered this. On one hand, Mina was not as powerful as Kelpie had thought, for she almost certainly could not read the crystal alone, and her magic message had failed to get through. But that was not to say she could not curse. Kelpie still had great faith in the power of Mina's evil spells. And Mina's curse would be even more disagreeable than her company. Kelpie brooded darkly over the unpleasant alternatives before her, almost inclined to risk the curse.

"Why would you not want to come?" demanded Mina, and her cursing changed to wheedling. "And here I have been to the trouble of arranging for you to learn witchcraft at last, ungrateful wretch that you are, then! What, would you stay to be a slave to arrogant fools such as these? Stupid sheep, spending their lives shut in a wee glen?"

"They do not, then," muttered Kelpie mutinously. "Ian and Alex have been to school in England in a place called Oxford, and have seen the King and Montrose and know more than we about affairs. And they do not beat me, nor make me steal for them and then set the crowd on me. And I do not believe you plan to teach me witchcraft, whatever, for you are always promising it and never do it."

Mina's face darkened, and she raised a scrawny, strong arm again, but Bogle loomed over her and drew her aside to speak for a moment in a voice like distant thunder. Kelpie watched apprehensively. When Bogle intervened, it was never for motives of kindness and charity.

"Hah!" Mina cackled presently and turned back to Kelpie. "And what of the wee bittie lass we were seeing you playing with so tenderly this morning? Shall I put a curse on her, too? Aye, on all the glen I shall put the Evil Eye, so that they will all wither up and die horrible deaths!"

Kelpie's defiance collapsed like a deflated bagpipe. Not Wee Mairi! She could not bear to risk harm for her bonnie bairn. But she must not let Mina know how vulnerable she was on this point, or she would be in slavery and Wee Mairi in danger forever more! Carefully keeping her face impassive, she shrugged indifferently. "Och, well, just do not be putting it on me," she murmured, and noted that both Mina and Bogle looked disappointed. "And will you truly be teaching me witchcraft if I come?" she demanded, as if this were her only interest.

"Have I not said so?" Mina growled. "Was it trying to drive a hard bargain you were, then? I should beat you for it! Come away down, now, for we have wasted too much time already." And she led the way down the hill.

It was the twins who first spotted the assorted trio approaching, and they began to shout excitedly.

"Kelpie, is yon your Grannie Witchie? Father, Ian, come and see!" they yelled in full voice. And then, short kilts swinging, they raced up the slope to stare at Mina and Bogle with frank, fearless curiosity.

"Are you truly a witch?" demanded Ronald, and, in spite of her gloom, Kelpie stifled a grin at the look on Mina's face.

The old woman drew herself up and glared at them. "Best not be asking that!" she warned in an ominous croak that should have completely cowed them, but didn't.

"Why not?" asked Ronald with great interest. "What will happen if we do? Do you not think, Donald, that she looks like a witch?"

"Ou, aye," declared Donald judiciously. "But we have not seen her casting any spells yet. Can you cast spells, Grannie Witchie?"

Kelpie's amusement changed to apprehension as the infuriated Mina spluttered speechlessly. It was probably only her speechlessness and the timely arrival of Glenfern that saved the twins from an awful fate. Mina gave them one last baleful glare—Kelpie fervently hoped it wasn't the Evil Eye—and turned to the tall chieftain. Kelpie glanced at him, and at Ian, Eithne, and Alex, who arrived just then from down by the loch, and then stared sullenly at the ground. She dared not look straight at them, for if they were to read her eyes and guess how she felt, then they would refuse to let her go, and so Mina's curse would be upon them. And now Kelpie found that her old misgivings were justified. She had recklessly given her affection and left herself vulnerable, so now she must suffer the consequences. Angrily she promised herself never to be so weak again.

"Well, then," said Glenfern pleasantly at last. "And are you leaving us, Kelpie?" She jerked her head, not looking at him. "I am sorry to hear it," he said gently, "for I think you were happy here, and we have come to like you well."

"Oh, Kelpie!" Eithne protested, shrinking a little from Mina and Bogle. "Can you not stay?"

"Och, you cannot go!" clamored the twins in outrage. "Who will be telling us stories now?"

Kelpie scowled, chewed her lip, and wished herself a thousand miles away. And worse was to come, for a brief glance upward showed her that all of them, from Mina to the twins, were on the verge of guessing her true feelings. She tossed her head and gave a hard little laugh. "Och, I'm away," she said airily, "for I've bided too long in one place."

Glenfern was looking at her keenly. "You are welcome to stay, you know," he told her.

"Aye, to slave for you without pay!" whined Mina in her most put-upon voice. If she had been slow to the attack, she made up for it now. "We have come to have her wages."

From under her lashes Kelpie saw the hurt on Eithne's face, and something like pity on Ian's. Only Alex wore a look of acid amusement that set Kelpie's teeth on edge. And Glenfern was giving Mina the same stern look he used when the twins had been naughty.

"I think you must be joking," he said quietly. "We have treated this lass far better than ever you have done. We have fed her properly, clothed her in decent, clean garments, taught her, given her affection and a roof over her head and a bed under her. What have you ever given her save harm and neglect?"

"She is ours!" Mina squealed angrily, but she must have seen that she would get nowhere, for she suddenly changed tactics. "Would you be wanting Mac Cailein Mor to hear things about you?" she hinted softly. "Things about how you are favoring King Charles, and what you think of the Covenant, and your own son associating with the King and bringing back messages from him, and from Montrose as well, perhaps?"

There was only one way Mina could have learned these things. Everyone looked at Kelpie, who stuck out her chin and grinned brazenly. Ou, the wicked, careless tongue of her, to be telling Mina that! Ian and Eithne were looking as if she had slapped them. There was a smile on Alex's lean face and scorn in his eyes.

"And so you have not really changed at all," he observed softly, and was surprised at the bitterness of his own disappointment. After all, what else had he expected? But his tongue went on scathingly. "Selfish, faithless, unscrupulous you are and always will be. You could never think of inconveniencing yourself for the good of another, could you, Kelpie?"

"Of course not," said Kelpie defiantly, but the sweet face of Wee Mairi was warm and mocking in her heart.

"Let be, Alex." Ian sighed. "She cannot help it. There was not enough time to change old habits."

"Nor ever will be," retorted Alex.

Kelpie hissed at him venomously. "Faithless yourself!" she spat. "Do not be forgetting what I told you, Ian!" And she turned away to Glenfern, who was laughing at Mina.

"By all means go to Argyll," he said cheerfully. "Tell him whatever you like. He knows well enough where our sympathies lie. But leave the lass behind you when you go, for I should not like her to be burned as a witch along with the two of you. And now, farewell. I am sorry," he added, turning to Kelpie, "that you could not stay with us, poor lass. Remember that we wish you well."

That was really almost too much. Kelpie turned abruptly and started up the pass with Mina and Bogle, who knew when they were defeated. At least it was over, and she must just put it away out of her memory.

But it was not quite over. Halfway up the hill a small

voice wailed after her. She turned to see Wee Mairi tugging at Eithne's hand, one small arm stretched out and upward. "My Kelpie!" she shrilled. "Do not go away, my Kelpie!"

Mina's pale eyes were upon Kelpie, narrowed, watchful, suspicious. Kelpie set her jaw, hardened her face, and deliberately turned her back on the broken-hearted little figure below.

The next few miles were blurred. Kelpie tramped mechanically behind Mina and Bogle, unseeing, trying to wipe three months out of her life and become the person she had been before. Och, she had been right to begin with! A feckless, foolish thing it was to care for anyone, and only hurt could come from it. From now on she would be hard as the granite sides of Ben Nevis, which now loomed ahead, snow still patching its sheer northern side. She would be what Alex thought her—and a pox on him, too. Nor would she even care that he would strike down that braw lad Ian, for Ian had had his warning, and it was his own fault if he was too stupid to heed it.

Scowling, she kicked at an inoffensive clump of bluebells and deliberately stepped on a wild yellow iris. She would become a witch, then; not a "coven witch," either. She had seen them—silly people, who made a great ceremony of selling their souls to the Devil and met in groups of thirteen, called covens, and held Black Mass, and did a great deal of wild dancing. Mina said these were little more than playing at witchcraft and learned only a few simple spells. No, now, Kelpie would be a witch of the old sort, who needed no bargains with Satan, but who tapped a Power that was old before the beginnings of Christianity. A Power it was that could be used for either black or white magic, but Kelpie had seen little of the white, and black seemed much more congenial, especially in her present mood.

She drifted into her old dream of what she would do one day to Mina and Bogle. Aye, and perhaps she would just add Alex as well. They were over the pass and heading south along the side of Loch Lochy before she came back to herself and began to wonder about the present.

"Where is it we are going now?" she demanded, moving up to walk beside Mina, half off the narrow path. "When will you be teaching me witchcraft? What are you planning?"

Mina cast a thoughtful eye at Kelpie's blue dress, now kilted up through her belt for easier walking. "I think that would be fitting me," she remarked casually. "We will be telling you what you will need to know when it is the right time for knowing it," she added so mildly that Kelpie looked at her with dark suspicion.

Falling behind once more, she began again to brood over her life. It consisted of being pushed from one situation into another. It was other folk who acted, and herself who reacted, who was acted upon. Was she, then, such a spineless creature? Was her whole life to be molded by others? Rebellion once more rose in her, but then subsided as she remembered the two-pronged stick that Mina held over her—nay, three-pronged, really. She could curse Kelpie, and she could curse Wee Mairi and Ian and the other folk of Glenfern, and only Mina could teach Kelpie witchcraft. And witchcraft, now, had become the only goal in her life, the only hope of escaping the hateful mastery of Mina and Bogle. Kelpie set her teeth, and the look on her face was neither pleasant nor attractive.

Down to the tip of Loch Lochy and on down the river they plodded, past the home of Glenfern's chief, Lochiel; and at last they made camp for the night in the old unfinished castle of Inverlochy. Roofless it was, and built foursquare, with a round tower at each corner, and Kelpie narrowed her eyes thoughtfully as they went in. Mina and Bogle never looked for walls about them, except sometimes in the cold of winter. What was afoot?

For the moment there was no time to wonder. Mina nodded brusquely at the river, which flowed just outside the arched stone entrance. "Gather us firewood," she ordered, "and then guddle us some fish—if you have not forgotten how." Her pale eyes rested again on Kelpie's dress, and Bogle chuckled.

An hour or so later, annoyed but not in the least astonished, Kelpie wiped her greasy fingers on the dirty rags

which now covered her, and glowered across the fire at
Mina. The hag and the blue dress were more or less the
same size, but of far different shapes. The dress sagged
across the front of Mina's hunched shoulders and strained
ominously across the back, and was at once too long and
too narrow in the waist, and the cuffs reached in vain for
those long bony wrists. Kelpie had a mental picture of
bright hazel eyes dancing in wicked amusement in an
angular red-topped face. For once she could have ap-
preciated Alex's sense of humor, and her own white teeth
showed momentarily in a matching grin.

Mina glared at her suspiciously, and Kelpie hastily
stopped grinning. *Dhé!* Mina was almost as bad as Alex
himself at seeing what she shouldn't! And she mustn't
anger Mina too much—not yet! So she lowered her slanted
eyes more or less submissively and waited.

"Hah!" said Mina suddenly. "You think I am not knowing what you are thinking?"

Kelpie devoutly hoped not. She had no desire to be
turned into a toad or something equally unpleasant. Best
to walk warily—neither too innocent nor too defiant.
"I am wondering what you are about," she retorted sullenly. "I have learned the things you were wanting me to,
but you have not told me why, nor have you taught me
any spells."

"Hah!" said Mina again. "First we will read the crystal."
And presently, under the ghost-light of the summer

night, Kelpie sat again with her hand in Mina's horny claw and gazed into the blank crystal ball. It remained still and empty. "I see myself," invented Kelpie impudently. "It is in a place that I have never been, and I am wearing a blue dress—"

Mina turned on her in sudden suspicion, and Kelpie prepared to duck. But they were distracted by a small flicker of light that came from an upper window of one of the castle towers. For an instant, fear gripped Kelpie. Was it an uncanny creature of some sort? Then she noticed that Bogle was nowhere in sight, and she chewed her lip thoughtfully.

Sure enough, presently his shadowy figure emerged from the tower door. He came back to the fire and sat down without a word. But Kelpie thought she had seen him put something in his new leather sporran (recently stolen, without doubt), and there passed between him and Mina a long look and the tiniest of nods.

Kelpie pretended to notice nothing, but her mind was busy. It couldn't have been magic he was up to, for Bogle did no magic except for ordinary curses. It must have been a message, then—a message left for him here, and they had known where to look for it. And that was why they camped in the castle instead of out in the open.

Och, there was something in the air, indeed and indeed! Kelpie went to sleep wondering what it might be—and how she might be turning it to her own advantage.

8. A Task for Kelpie

FROM Inverlochy Castle they headed southeast, around the tip of Loch Leven and into the lands of the Stewarts of Glencoe. Now they definitely turned southward. Kelpie frowned.

"Will we be going into Campbell country, then?" she asked, faintly alarmed. For the last time they had ventured into Argyll's lands there had been an all too exciting witch hunt from which they had barely escaped, so it must be an important matter indeed that would bring Mina and Bogle back again into danger.

Mina just grunted disagreeably, but by the next day Kelpie's question was answered, for they reached Loch Etive, which was well into Campbell land. Mina glanced around nervously, and Kelpie again wondered where they were going, and why. Bogle stood for a moment, staring down the loch, then turned and purposefully led the way to the precise spot where the River Etive entered the northernmost tip. Clearly he knew exactly where he was going. And then Kelpie saw what must be the reason for this journey. A man sat waiting for them in a copse of alder near the river, looking oddly out of place in the sober gray breeches of a Lowlander.

"Aweel," he said and looked at them. Kelpie's sharp eyes took in every detail of the stocky long-armed figure, with sandy hair cropped to its ears, and sandy eyebrows looking too thin for the broad face. She did not like what she saw, and even less what she felt. For there was no expression at all on the Lowlander's face. His eyes were like cold pebbles, and there was a malignance about him that made her shrink inside.

Suddenly Kelpie knew that he must be a warlock. Mina and Bogle would not be merely working with him; they were under his orders. Probably it was he who was behind Mina's interest in politics, Kelpie's long stay at Glenfern, this hurried trip. Och, it was a powerful and evil man, this, and she would do well to fear him.

The small opaque eyes studied her for a moment and then turned to Mina, who looked small and shrunken before them. "Is yon the lass?" Their owner demanded in the burred English of Glasgow.

Mina nodded, and the eyes turned back to Kelpie. "Come here!" he commanded.

Kelpie had a passionate desire to assert her own will

and refuse. But it would be daft to try to challenge his power now—and especially with Mina and Bogle watching her. Reluctantly, her own eyes smoldering with anger and foreboding, she went and stood before him, and he seemed to read her thoughts.

"So, ye'd like tae be a witch," he said, his voice half a sneer, half a caress. "Tae hae sich power, ye maun learn tae obey. Obey! Ye didna ken that, eh? Weel—ailbins ye can prove yersel' the noo, and earn the powers ye're wanting." He turned to Mina again. "Hae ye told her?"

Mina shook her head humbly. "Never a word."

"Good. She'll hear it the noo," returned the Lowlander. He turned back to Kelpie, whose small face regarded him with wary intensity. His face became genial and fatherly. "Ye're a lucky lass," he began, "tae hae us a' so concerned wi' yer ain guid."

Kelpie laughed aloud, and there was genuine amusement as well as derision in her laughter. Did they think her a bairn, and daft as well?

At once the Lowlander became brisk and businesslike. Very well, then, he conceded, perhaps it was not merely her own good they were after. But she would profit greatly. Who, he demanded, was her worst enemy?

Kelpie prudently did not name Mina and Bogle. Instead, she remembered Mina's deep interest of late and made a shrewd guess at the answer he expected. "Mac Cailein Mor?"

"Aye, Argyll," he said approvingly and went on to point out why. The Kirk of the Covenant was reaching farther and farther into the Highlands now, with its persecution of honest witches, and even of stupid old folk who were not witches at all, for that matter. And who was head of the Covenant? Who was spearhead of the persecutions, the pricking and torture and burnings? Argyll. If he was not stopped, there would be no safe place in all Scotland for such as they.

Kelpie nodded and found part of her mind thinking that on this one point only—Argyll and the Covenant— did her world and that of Glenfern agree.

Very well, then, the Lowlander continued. They must take steps to destroy Argyll. And what better thing than a hex? A wee image of him, in clay or wax, they would make. And then they would stick pins in it, roast it, freeze it, pour poison over it, and, by the black powers of witch- craft, all these things would happen to Mac Cailein Mor himself, until at last he would die in great pain.

Again Kelpie nodded warily. And how did she enter into all this, at all?

She found out soon enough. In order to make a really effective hex on Argyll, something from himself was needed to mold into the wax figure—hair or fingernail clippings, preferably. And who was to obtain them? Why, Kelpie, of course.

Now it was clear why she had been left at Glenfern to

learn the ways of gentry and how to be a servant. She
would hire herself as housemaid at Inverary Castle and,
as soon as she managed to get the hair or fingernail clippings, just come away back here with them. And as a
reward she would be taught all she wished to know about
spells, potions, curses—even the Evil Eye itself.

As easy as that!

They were making her their tool again, of course, to
do what they dared not do themselves. If she were caught,
her life would not be worth a farthing. Still—Kelpie
thought quickly behind narrowed eyes and an impassive
face. It was a chance to get away from Mina and Bogle
and perhaps take a hand in managing her own life. Once
away in Inverary, she could decide whether or not to carry
out the errand. Perhaps she would prefer Mac Cailein Mor
to Mina and just stay for a while. Or perhaps . . . Well,
she would see.

She listened with great docility as they explained how
she could get in touch with them once she had completed
her task. She even nodded when the Lowlander suggested
blandly that it might just be safest to send the hair—or
half of it—on to them by the messenger they would tell
her of, and then she herself could be bringing the rest
later. Kelpie kept a sneer from crossing her face. If they
thought her so witless as that, let them, then! But if and
when she came to them, it would be with the hair hidden

in a safe place, and they having to fulfill their part of the bargain before they saw it.

The Lowlander was very pleased with her, and Kelpie went to bed very pleased with herself. But she awoke near dawn with the sense of something bothering her.

The sky was a vast aching void, neither black nor light. The world was a great shadow. Kelpie crept silently away from the camp and over the crest of the nearest rise, still wrapped in the old woolen plaidie which served as cloak and blanket. She seated herself against the thickness of a rhododendron, so that she was lost in the black shadows of its great leaves and blossoms. Then she stared down along the long, steely sheet of Loch Etive and began to think.

Obey, the Lowlander had said—and clearly Mina and Bogle were obeying him. But Kelpie had thought that to be a witch was to be free, to have power to command others, never to *be* commanded again by anyone.

Was it not so, after all? Did the Lowlander, in turn, obey someone—or Something? For an instant Kelpie sensed something infinitely dangerous and horrible. Was Satan merely another name for those ancient Dark Powers? And was the price for invoking them to be a slave to them? She shuddered, and cold droplets of sweat broke out on her short upper lip.

Then she pulled herself together. She must not give in

to foolish worries. The Lowlander was a fearsome man, but witchcraft was the only way to be free of Mina, and when she had learned it she need fear neither of them any longer.

All the same, the first seed of doubt had taken root, and it no longer seemed quite so easy to become the most powerful witch in Scotland. It was a rather subdued Kelpie who meekly cooked the fish and oatcakes for breakfast, bade the Lowlander farewell, and followed Bogle and Mina on to Loch Awe.

At a ruined old shieling hut by the loch they stopped and waited for a day, until there came a round-faced young woman with a wealth of brown hair and a slate-colored dress kilted up over a striped petticoat. She seemed an unlikely person to be working with witches and warlocks, for her bright-cheeked smile was quite artless.

"Dhia dhuit!" She beamed. "Is this the lass who will be fetching the hair to hex Mac Cailein Mor, may the demons fly away with him? I am Janet Campbell, who will take you to Inverary. I will call you Sheena at once," she added chattily, "so you can get used to it, for Mrs. MacKellar would never be hiring a lass named for a kelpie." She chuckled cheerfully.

Kelpie gave her an appraising look from under her thick black lashes, but Janet didn't seem in the least put out. "I could not be doing the task myself," she explained, "for I have my work, and no reason to be going into the castle.

And," she added forthrightly, "I am not brave or clever enough. But I will be your messenger, Sheena, when you need me."

Kelpie, more and more resentful of being used by others, nodded sullenly. But Janet's next words cheered her considerably.

"She cannot be asking for work in such rags," pointed out that young woman matter-of-factly. "They would know her for a gypsy at once, and Mac Cailein Mor has a fearful hatred of such. Best be giving her your blue dress to wear, Mina."

Bogle chuckled, and Kelpie hid her satisfaction behind a blank face. Mina snarled and gave in. The string of epithets she flung at Kelpie along with the dress hardly amounted to an objection at all, and Kelpie's earlier misgivings rose again briefly. If even the formidable Mina was so meekly obeying, then what power this Lowlander must have!

She was still brooding on this as she and Janet set out on the last bit of the journey, her cheek still stinging from Mina's farewell cuff. On down Loch Awe, and to the wild steepness of Glen Aray, and along that gash in the hills toward Loch Fyne, Janet led the way sturdily enough, although Kelpie's wiry legs could have gone much faster. Part of the time Janet left the thin path altogether and threaded her way along the slopes, among great clumps of brilliant pink rhododendron, groves of oak and hazel and rowan, patches of lavender-blooming heath and the mystic white bog-cotton.

"Best not to risk meeting anyone," she remarked with a trace of nervousness. "I dare not be seen with you, in case . . ."

She left the sentence unfinished and went on in a new and brisk voice. "Now I will be giving you your story to tell the housekeeper when you ask for work. You are Sheena Campbell, daughter to Sorcha and Seumas, who lived in the old shieling hut where we met on Loch Awe. When they died, you went in service with MacIntyre of Craignish, but now, with their daughter wedded and away, there is no need for you. So you have come to Inverary, to your own clan chief, to see is there a place for you."

For the next two hours she fed Kelpie the details of her fictional life and made her repeat them over and over, until Kelpie almost felt that she was two people at once.

"Och, you're glib, just!" said Janet at last, her round face admiring. "I'm almost believing you myself. 'Tis a clever mind you have, and a canny tongue." She stopped and turned around to survey Kelpie's face searchingly. "Aye," she went on, "and your face, though it is not bonnie, just, is a face to beguile the lads. Have you a braw laddie who loves you, Sheena?"

Four months ago Kelpie would have jeered at her in

wonder and scorn. What had the lass of Mina and Bogle to do with love, or lads either—save to sell love-charms to the foolish? But though there had been no talk or thought of romance at Glenfern (except on one teasing afternoon), some sleeping thing in Kelpie had, perhaps, begun to stir. The face of Ian leaped into her mind, with the fine dark eyes of him, and the sensitive mouth curving downward and then up; and then she felt the strange, warm-faced sensation of her first blush—and she felt again the pain of her departure from Glenfern.

"No!" She spat so violently that Janet raised her eyebrows and gave Kelpie another sharp glance before she turned to walk on.

"A pity, that," she observed mildly. "And a great waste," she added presently, with a catch to her voice. "Had I your face and tongue, I would not be in the service of witchcraft, perhaps."

Kelpie kilted up her blue dress a bit higher and came even with Janet so that she could see her face. "Why are you?" she demanded curiously. "I think you could never be a witch."

"Och, no!" agreed Janet instantly. "At first I was only wanting a wee bit of a love potion to win the heart of the lad I loved. But before it could start to work at all, Mac Cailein Mor took him into the army and off to raid the MacDonalds. Och, my braw Angus." She whimpered.

"He was killed?" Kelpie asked, and tried to push down the sympathy in her voice. She had promised herself not to care for anyone again, but only for herself.

"It was Mac Cailein Mor had him shot," said Janet tonelessly. "He tried to save an old woman from the house they were burning. And for that I will help the Devil himself to destroy Mac Cailein Mor, my chief though he be. I am afraid of yon Lowlander, for he is evil, but I hate Mac Cailein Mor more than I fear the Lowlander."

"You must be very canny, Sheena! If you are caught—" She shuddered. "Have you a *sgian dhu?*"

Kelpie nodded and drew the small sheathed knife from inside her dress. Janet looked at it somberly. "If you're caught, you'd do well to use it on yourself. 'Twould save you torment and burning, more than likely, and keep you from betraying the rest of us. You'll say no word, ever, about me, Sheena? Pretend you have never seen or heard of me! Promise, Sheena!"

Kelpie looked at her, and Janet's eyes were humble and pleading. "I know I am a coward," Janet whispered, "but I cannot help it. I could not bear the pain, and I would not dare to kill myself—but you would, for you are brave."

Kelpie looked at her *sgian dhu* reflectively. It was the finest one she had ever had, the one stolen last spring in Inverness. The wee flat scabbard was darkly carved, and the four-inch blade, when she drew it out, winked sharply in the sun. Would she use it on herself? she wondered. Did she dare?

The beauty of the Highlands shimmered around her in pure, clear colors never quite the same from one instant to the next. The sky was infinite and tender; the sun beat warmly on her head; the air was delight to breathe. The world was good—except for the people in it, defiling it with hate and greed. It would be a pity to die, a waste of living. She found it very difficult to imagine.

She looked again at the gleaming edge of the *sgian dhu,* frowning a little. Dare? Yes, she thought she would dare, if it was to escape torture and burning. That would not take much courage. On the contrary, it would be the easy way—and she found that she did not like the taste of the idea. A feeling within her protested that suicide was shabby, debasing, a cheating of oneself. But Kelpie, who had never been taught such things as morals and integrity, could find no words and no reasons for this feeling. She shrugged and put the *sgian dhu* back. Time enough to think about it if the occasion came up.

Janet had been watching her with round eyes, guessing a little of her thought. She shivered slightly. "You are very brave," and said again. "I think you will be getting away with the hair. And I am sure that whatever is happening at all, you will not speak any names."

Kelpie fell back a step or two. She looked thoughtfully

on a golden patch of gorse blanketing the hillside ahead, and her smile was very pointed. No, she would not betray Janet—not, she reminded herself, because she was softhearted, but only because it would not help herself. But—if she was so unlucky as to be caught, which she did not at all intend to be—she would be very happy indeed to tell Mac Cailein Mor all about Mina, Bogle, and the Lowlander.

9. Inverary Castle

Loch Fyne stretched long and narrow between its hills —as what Highland loch did not? Glen Aray opened out into a meadow there, where the river entered the loch, and from the top of her hill Kelpie had a fine and leisurely view. There was the town of Inverary on the far side, nestled right on the loch. And on this side, almost below her, rose the massive stone bulk and towers of Inverary Castle, home of Mac Cailein Mor.

Kelpie wriggled a little deeper into her nest of tall harebells and broom and stared down at it with interest. She had time to wait and think. Janet had braided the black hair neatly for her, used the hem of her own dress to wash Kelpie's grimy pointed face, and then hurried on to the head of the loch. From there she would return to the village as if from her own home. And Kelpie was to bide here, out of sight, until the next day, and then come down from the glen. Kelpie had agreed willingly enough, not for Janet's sake, but for one more night under the free sky.

She glowered at the brooding gray castle, for it was just occurring to her that it would be much more like a prison than Glenfern. And would they allow her to be out and away in the hills when her tasks were done, as she had done at Glenfern? She doubted it. Och, it was a great sacrifice she was making for those who had sent her, and she must see that her reward was as great. And then . . . She drifted into her favorite daydream.

In the long white twilight she backed down the hill until she found a tarn sheltered by birch, and settled herself for the night. The Dancers were absent tonight, and the sky a pale shadowed silver in which only the largest stars flickered feebly, for it was midsummer. Then the moon came over the crest of the hill, and there were no more stars, and the tarn became a pool of cold light. Deliberately Kelpie leaned over the bank and stared into the tarn.

The reflected brilliance of moonlight glowed, closed in upon itself, became a silver point, and then in its place there was a strange land—a place with giant forests, dark and wild, and a crude house made of logs in a rough clearing. She tossed her head with annoyance. What was this to her? What of her future, her career as a witch? What of destruction of those she hated? What of her enemies?

The tarn obeyed, as if with a malicious will of its own, and she saw Argyll's face, the eyes coldly burning, the mouth twisted in anger, staring straight at her, and in her mind's ear Kelpie heard the word "witch."

She threw herself backward and sat with beating heart for several moments after the water stood clear and blank. Was she fey, then? Was it her own doom she was seeing? Och, no, perhaps not. For she had not seen herself, and surely Mac Cailein Mor had looked so to many a person accused of witchcraft. She had asked to see her enemy, and the picture was telling her, just, that here was a dangerous enemy—a warning to be canny, that was all. She curled up comfortably in a patch of rank grass free of nettles, and slept.

In the thin light of morning she smoothed back her hair and washed her face in the cold, peaty water of the tarn. Then, wary but confident, she made her way back to the glen and along the river to the castle.

As she approached the massive stone gateway, Kelpie put on the proper face and attitude for this occasion as easily as Eithne might have put on a different frock. The task was not so easy, really, for there was little that could be done about the long slanted eyes and brows or the pointed jaw. But the severely braided hair helped, and by tucking in her lower lip and drooping the corners she added a helpless and wistful note. She pulled her chin down and back and pressed her elbows to her sides for a look of brave apprehension, and then she changed her free, fawnlike walk for a most sober one.

Through the gate she stepped into a subdued world of drab colors. Her blue dress looked insolently bright beside the grays and blacks of the other women in the courtyard. Only the tartan—that proud symbol of the Highlander— had failed to be extinguished by the decree of the Covenant and Kirk. And even the tartans, being colored with vegetable dye, were of muted shades.

A man leading a horse stopped and regarded her with little approval. "What is it that you are wanting?" he asked.

"Could I be seeing Mrs. MacKellar, the housekeeper?" asked Kelpie, her eyes lowered modestly.

He looked at her for a moment and then called over his shoulder, "Siubhan, the lass is wanting Mrs. MacKellar. Take her away up to the door." And he went on about his business.

A sad-faced woman put down her basket of laundry, regarded Kelpie without curiosity, and jerked her head. Kelpie followed with great meekness and waited obediently at the castle door until Siubhan had gone inside and reappeared with a tall, gaunt woman in black.

Once again there was the disapproving look. "And who may you be?"

"I be Sheena Campbell." Kelpie launched into her story,

not too glibly, with downcast eyes and humble voice. "And it's hoping I am to serve Mac Cailein Mor," she finished earnestly.

"Mmmm," commented Mrs. MacKellar. "We've lasses aplenty in Inverary Village."

"Och," protested Kelpie, "but 'tis experience I've had! And," she added pitifully, "they will be having homes, and I with nowhere to turn."

Mrs. MacKellar softened, but only slightly. "To tell the truth," she said bluntly, "there is something—I'm not altogether liking the look of you! How am I knowing you are what you say?"

"But and whyever else would I be coming to Mac Cailein Mor?" demanded Kelpie artlessly.

"Mmmm, that will be the question," retorted Mrs. Mac-Kellar. "No, now, I'm thinking—"

What she thought was never said, for from the corner of her eye Kelpie saw a tall figure just passing the foot of the stairs—not Argyll, but his tallness, his long face, red hair, and manner of dress suggested that he must be Argyll's son. Kelpie took a chance.

She turned away blindly from the imminent refusal, carefully stumbled a bit, and tumbled herself neatly down the steps to land in a pathetic heap in front of the startled young man.

"My sorrow!" he ejaculated.

Kelpie swiftly decided against being injured, as this

might prove inconvenient. So she gave a small scared glance upward at the faint frown above her and shrank back against the wall. "Och, your pardon!" she whispered. "Please do not be beating me!"

The young man—she was quite sure now that he must be Lord Lorne, son of Argyll—gave a short laugh. "Whatever you may have heard, I am no beater of bairns."

Kelpie drooped her lip at him. "Sir, I would not mind a beating, if only I could be staying here to work for Mac Cailein Mor."

"What is this? Who is she?" Lord Lorne switched to English, and Mrs. MacKellar replied in the same tongue.

"She iss saying her name iss Sheena Campbell from Loch Awe, and that she iss an orphan who hass peen working in the home of MacIntyre of Craignish who iss not needing her any more." Mrs. MacKellar's English, sibilant with the soft Gaelic sounds, was really not nearly as good as Kelpie's—but Kelpie was careful to keep her face blank, as if she did not understand. "But sir," went on the housekeeper, "I am not liking the look of her whateffer. Her eyes—"

Lord Lorne bent and looked at them. Kelpie tried to make them wide and pleading.

"Oddly ringed, aren't they?" he observed. "Well, she can't help that. You could use her, I think. Why not try her out?" And he went on to wherever he had been going.

"*Seadh.*" Mrs. MacKellar shrugged and washed her

hands of the decision. "You can be staying a bit, then, until I see can you do the work. We will see does Peigi have an old dress you can be wearing, of a proper color. You're of the Kirk, are you no?" she demanded suddenly, turning to cast a suspicious eye on the blue of Kelpie's dress.

Kelpie wasn't quite sure what that meant, and, even with Janet's tutoring, she dared not bluff too far. She took an instant to think as she rose slowly to her feet. "I am wanting to be a better Christian," she said, temporizing, with an earnest face. "And that is one reason I was coming here, for the house of Mac Cailein Mor is surely the most godly of all."

"Well—" Mrs. MacKellar looked somewhat appeased. "Come away in, then." And Kelpie came.

Life in Inverary Castle was quite different from life at Glenfern, even though Kelpie's duties were similar. There was a coldness here—and not only physical, although the castle was chill enough, with draughts constantly blowing down the halls and pushing out against the wall tapestries. But the chill of spirit was even more depressing. Laughter was near sacrilege, and a smile darkly suspect. Dancing simply didn't exist, and singing was confined to dour hymns regarding hellfire and damnation. If Kelpie had ever chafed at the restrictions of Glenfern, she now realized what a free and happy life that had been. Och, that

people could live like this! Worse, that they seemed to
approve it! One could hardly say they *liked* anything.

And here Kelpie heard the other viewpoint regarding
Mac Cailein Mor. Everyone seemed to fear him, even his
rather mousy wife and sullen son. But they also saw him
(except possibly Lord Lorne) as the Right Hand of God,
fighting the battles of righteousness against such enemies
of Heaven as witches, King Charles, Papists, Anglicans,
everyone else who was not of the Covenant, and, most
particularly, Lord Graham of Montrose, who was sup-
posedly leading the King's army in Scotland. But no one
seemed to know where Montrose was now, at all. He had
started north to raise an army for the king and then vanished altogether, and it was to be fondly hoped that the
Devil had snatched him away to Hell where he belonged.

Kelpie listened and said nothing. She didn't like what
she heard and began to hate Argyll on her own account.
Indeed and it was true that he would take all freedom
from all people if he could. Kelpie cared little enough
about anyone else, she told herself, but her own freedom
mattered more than anything at all, and she began to feel
a personal enthusiasm for her task here. A hex was what
he deserved, and she hoped that the Lowlander would
make it a fine horrible one indeed.

It was lucky, she discovered, that himself was home at
all now, for he spent much of his time these days heading
his Covenant army, raiding the Highlands, and occasion-

ally daring a small skirmish with other enemies. (Kelpie received the impression that he was not, perhaps, the boldest and most audacious leader when it came to fighting.) But now he was home, as no doubt the Lowlander had known.

Still, three bleak weeks had passed, and she still had never had a chance to lay her hands on any bit of his person or even come near his private rooms. Mrs. Mac-Kellar kept a watchful eye out, and Kelpie's duties were confined to all wings of the castle but that of Mac Cailein Mor. And so she watched and waited through June, tense, wary, inwardly chafing.

10. A Bit of Hair

IT WAS an impossible errand they had sent her on! Kelpie realized it slowly, angrily. A bit of Argyll's hair, indeed and indeed! Nobody at all would be so feckless as to leave a bit of his hair lying about, convenient to the hand of any witch who happened to be passing. And how much less Mac Cailein Mor, who was thrice as crafty, ten times as suspicious, and a thousand times more hated than most folk? Och, no; for him such carelessness would be altogether impossible. It was certain that he would stand over his barber while every last hair or fingernail clipping was safely burned. The best she could hope for was a bit of his personal belongings, which would be much less effective; and whatever Mina and the Lowlander would say she did not know. No doubt they would make an excuse to refuse to teach her spells, after all.

And so she seethed under the joyless Covenant mask

which was becoming harder and harder to wear. How she
longed for the freedom of the open! Her legs ached with
the longing to run and leap and dance upon the hills, and
her face ached with the need to laugh. And yet she stayed
on, hoping for some miracle, reflecting sourly that Mrs.
MacKellar and Argyll were very little improvement over
Mina and Bogle.

It was in mid-July that it happened, during morning
prayer.

Kelpie knelt with the rest of the household on the cold
stone floor in grim endurance, for this long, twice-daily
torment was nearly unbearable for an active young gypsy.

Her place was in the very back, among the meanest of
the servants. Ahead, the bowed backs graduated in rank,
with Mrs. MacKellar far up front, just behind meek Lady
Argyll, Lord Lorne, and Ewen Cameron, whose red kilt
blazed sharply alien amid all the blue and green of the
Campbell tartan. And before them all stood Mac Cailein
Mor's long, stooped figure, telling of the anger, jealousy,
cruelty of a God who could surely have nothing to do
with the opal world outside. With cold satisfaction and
in grim detail he described God's will (which seemed in-
distinguishable from Argyll's will); and his pale eyes were
most disconcerting, for if one seemed fixed upon Siubhan
or Peigi, the other seemed to stare straight at Kelpie, and
who was to know what himself was really looking at,
whatever?

"Behold, the day of Jehovah cometh, cruel, with wrath and fierce anger; to make the land a desolation, and to destroy the sinners thereof out of it," said Argyll. "He shall destroy the minions of Satan, those evildoers who are not of the Kirk, who blasphemously question the Covenant. For all those who are not with the Covenant are against the Lord and vile in His sight. They shall burn forever in Hell, and above all shall burn all witches and that servant of the Devil, Montrose. They shall be tormented—"

Kelpie felt the presence of the messenger in the open door behind her, but dared not turn to look. She saw Argyll's eye flicker briefly in that direction and noticed the slight pause before he went coldly on with his orders to and from God. And something inside Kelpie stirred, and she knew that something was about to happen which would be important to her.

Dropping her dark head over clasped hands in an attitude of great reverence, she tried to think what it could be. There was nothing she had done. Unless— Had Ewen Cameron said something about yesterday?

For yesterday Kelpie had found her first opportunity to get away over to the wing which held the chambers of Mac Cailein Mor and his family. She had actually reached his door, and as she hesitated there, heart beating quickly, another door nearby had opened, and through it came a lad of about fifteen.

Kelpie had not needed to look at the oddness of a Cameron tartan in the Campbell stronghold to know that this was Ewen, the grandson of Lochiel. Ian had told her about him, and she had seen him now and again about the castle. And Peigi had told her proudly how fine it was that Mac Cailein Mor was taking on himself the education of his nephew, for fear it should be neglected or his own family should teach him to believe the wrong things.

Kelpie had hidden a cynical smile at the time, but now, when the grave, clear-eyed lad stood regarding her in the hall, she wondered briefly how much this "education" would really mean. For he had about him the air of one with a mind of his own.

"You'll be Sheena, will you not?" he asked as Kelpie belatedly made a stiff bob. She nodded. "Best not to linger here," he went on. "If my uncle should see you—"

"Aye," Kelpie had murmured, and slipped away back to her own territory with the odd feeling that he had seen through her mask—not, perhaps, that he knew exactly what was under it, but that he knew she was alien to this world of Inverary.

Could he have said anything, just? Kelpie wondered as she shifted her knees ever so slightly on the painfully hard stone. The thing inside said no. He was another of those strange people, like Ian and Eithne, who seemed not to hate anyone or even wish them ill.

But still, something was about to happen, and she must find out as soon as ever she could. When prayers were over, and the household rose and respectfully made way for himself to go out first, it was easy enough for her to slip nearest the door, for she had had a wealth of experience at picking pockets and melting through crowds. And so she saw the travel-weary messenger waiting outside, and heard the news when Argyll did.

"Antrim of Colonsay and his clan of Irish MacDonalds have landed at Ardnaburchen and taken the castle of Mingary, and will even now be taking the keep of Lochaline, your Lordship!"

The Marquis of Argyll said something under his breath, and the freckles suddenly stood out under the red hair that Kelpie coveted. "May the Devil take his impudence!" he said aloud, and there was no doubt that he meant it literally.

Kelpie tried to remember something she had heard at Glenfern. Antrim—Colkitto, they called him—was chief of a branch of MacDonalds that the Campbells had driven westward, over the islands, and at last to Ireland. And now, it seemed, he had decided to bring his clan back to Scotland to fight the Campbells and perhaps take back some land.

"Have messengers ready to ride," Argyll said viciously to his son. "I'll have the army up and wipe him out once and for all!" By this time the rest of the household had filtered out into the hall, and it didn't seem to matter if they all heard or no. But then, there'd be no keeping this kind of news secret, whatever.

Kelpie clenched her fists. We? Then would Mac Cailein Mor be away with the army himself?

"Isn't there an English Parliament garrison at Carlisle?" ventured Lord Lorne in English. "Why not send to them to take warships up the coast? If they captured Antrim's ships, there'd be no retreat for him."

Argyll nodded brusquely and strode off toward his chambers to write the necessary letters—taking his hair with him, of course. "Get my things ready to ride," he ordered one of his retainers, thus destroying Kelpie's last hope.

"*Dhé!*" she muttered, without changing the blank and sober expression considered suitable for God-fearing people. Whatever could she be doing now, at all, with him away?

Impulsively, she slipped out of the hall before Mrs. MacKellar or Peigi should see her, and made her way to the tower next to Argyll's wing. There she hid her thin self partway up the steep, twisting stairs, where with one eye she could see his door, and waited. Not that he would be likely to be trimming his hair or fingernails now, but perhaps in the flurry of his leaving she could just slip in and lay hold of some wee personal item to be used instead, and it the best she could do.

It was a full half-hour before Argyll's door opened. Kelpie glimpsed the full tartan folds of his belted plaid and then pressed herself out of sight as the halting steps assured her that it was indeed Mac Cailein Mor.

She waited until they had passed down the hall and out of hearing, and then slipped out of the tower and across to the massive oaken door. She paused an instant, hand lifted to open the door, but it was almost certain there could be no one else in there, for the entire household had been at morning prayer, and no one else had gone in. The door opened heavily, with never a creak, and closed firmly behind her.

Here must be his Lordship's private withdrawing room. Kelpie had never seen such a room, and she glanced around with interest. The clan crest, a boar's head, was carved over the large stone fireplace and on the back of the high oaken settle that stood at one wall. A bulky armchair with a triangular seat going to a point in back stood by a long table on which quills, ink, sand, and paper still stood. But there was nothing personal. His bedroom must be on through that other door.

She darted across the room silently, opened the door, and saw an enormous four-post bedstead of inlaid walnut —a fine piece indeed, she thought cynically, for an unworldly Covenanter! No less than three great-chests doubtless held his clothing and perhaps Lady Argyll's—but clothing would be too bulky for Kelpie's needs. A plaid-brooch might just do nicely, though, and they should be in a cupboard, perhaps, or a wee box somewhere.

Kelpie began investigating. And then she nearly yelped with triumph. A brush! A brush in which were tangled several long strands of red hair! Och, and he *had* been careless, then, perhaps with being upset from the news of Antrim. Och, the fine luck of it! Chuckling, she pulled them loose, looked around for something to wrap them in —and saw the bedroom door swing inexorably open.

There he stood, Mac Cailein Mor, one eye regarding her balefully, the other apparently fixed on the wall behind; and the thin lips were pitiless. For once Kelpie's quick mind and glib tongue failed her altogether, and she just stood there while he crossed the room in three strides and seized her wrist.

"A thief, is it?" he rasped.

Kelpie found her wits. "Och, no, your worship!" she cried. "I know it's no right I have to be coming here, but it's the fine and godly man you are, and leaving now, and I just wanting to see—"

He pried her hand roughly open, and the damning evidence of the hairs lay exposed on her palm.

"A witch!" he said with savage glee. "A witch in my own household. Ah, the Devil is trying hard to destroy me, for I do the work of the Lord. Blessed are those who are persecuted for Thy name's sake. Spawn of Satan, do you know what we do with witches?"

"Witches?" faltered Kelpie with desperate innocence, though she knew by now that pretense was hopeless. Far less evidence than this would have been fatal, and even with a much less suspicious man than Mac Cailein Mor. Sudden hot anger almost drove out her terror for an instant —not so much at Argyll as at Mina and Bogle and the Lowlander, who had so callously sent her on this errand. They had surely known how slim her chances were, and that she would almost certainly be caught and burned. And they would never have taught her the Evil Eye, even had she been successful. She had been their tool and cat's-paw, and she cursed herself for being such a fool. Och, she would see to it before she died that Argyll knew their names and the meeting place.

She didn't once think of the *sgian dhu* that rested within the bodice of her sober gray dress.

Mac Cailein Mor was dragging her out of the room, baying for his servants, the dangerous hairs safely in his own hand. Kelpie submitted passively because it would do no good at all to struggle. Her mind darted here and there, like a moth in a glass ball, finding no way out at all.

And now all the household was running, and two husky men took her from Argyll and hustled her brutally through the castle and out to the courtyard, while Argyll sputtered his tale to his son between bellows for Mrs. MacKellar.

"Was it you hired her?" he demanded ominously of the

cringing housekeeper. "Could you not see the eyes of her, the teeth, the brows? Or was it yourself plotting against me too? Are the minions of Satan filling my own home?" He was working himself into a fine frenzy, and even through her terror Kelpie found time to wonder briefly at the idiotic honesty of Lorne, who spoke up then.

" 'Twas my fault, Father. Mrs. MacKellar didn't like the look of the lass when she came to ask for employment, and I was fool enough to feel sorry for her, and I said to take her in." He met his sire's black glare straight. " 'Twas stupid," he said firmly, "but no plot against you by any here."

"The Devil addled your wits, then," retorted Argyll, not to be deprived of his martyrdom. "Could you not see the ringed eyes of her? No, do not look into them! She'll cast a spell!" He glared at Lorne, and then, dourly, at Ewen Cameron, who stood near with an expressionless face.

Kelpie was again fervently wishing that she *could* cast a spell! Och, the plague she would be putting on the lot of them, and himself in particular! Since she couldn't, she tucked in her lower lip, lowered the offensive eyes, hung meekly in the painful grip on her arms, and made one last hopeless try for her life.

"What was it I was doing wrong?" she whimpered. "It was nothing valuable I was taking, but only a wee bit token to protect me from the Devil whilst yourself was away."

It was no use at all. Everyone knew what hairs were used for, even children.

"Shall we burn her now, Mac Cailein Mor?" asked one of the men. Kelpie's heart thudded sickly. But Argyll brooded.

"No time now," he said reluctantly. "I'll be wanting to test her for witch marks and get a full confession and the names of her accomplices. And there's Antrim to deal with first." He looked frustrated at having to delay, and Kelpie realized that here was a man who enjoyed cruelty for its own sake. She shuddered.

"Put her in the dungeon," ordered Argyll, "the wee cell at the bottom, and with no blanket. And let no one open the door or speak to her until I return. Put bread and water through the grate, but nothing else. Is everything ready, Buchanan? My horse, then."

He turned away, and Kelpie drew a small shaky breath. A wee respite, then, and perhaps a chance to escape altogether from the torture and burning, if they didn't search her and take away the *sgian dhu*—and if she made up her mind to use it.

11. Argyll's Dungeon

THE cell was tiny, damp, cold, and inconceivably black. Within ten minutes after the solid door thudded behind her, Kelpie was cowering on the floor. Even an ordinary roof was oppressive to her, and this— Ou, the dark and the smallness were almost tangible things that seemed to press down and in on her, smothering and squashing! It was even hard to breathe, just with the thinking of it.

By the time half an hour had passed, it was all she could do not to shriek wildly and beat her head against the stone. She gritted her teeth, sensing that self-control was her only hold on sanity. How could mere darkness hurt the eyes so? Kelpie began fingering her *sgian dhu* longingly. It was escape, escape from this torment and that to follow. She had no great fear of death, in spite of all she had heard of Hell, for at worst it was almost certain to be interesting.

And yet, the thing inside would not let her use the wee sharp dagger that nestled so temptingly in her hand. It gave no reason, except that this was a mean and shabby way to die.

For nearly the first time in her memory, Kelpie cried. On and on she sobbed, for as space was closing in on her, time was stretched into a long and empty void, and she was alone in chaos and terror.

Once she thought that perhaps if she did kill herself now, her Hell would be an eternity of this, and she shuddered at the thought. Argyll's God might just do such a thing, and Satan's fire was surely to be preferred—but which of them would be having the decision, at all? Her thoughts blurred off into confusion.

Some time later a grate in the door opened, a hand pushed a bit of bread through the pale oblong, and it clanged shut again. Kelpie roused herself to explore the spot with her long, sensitive fingers but found it small and solidly bolted. She took a few halfhearted bites of bread and lapsed again into a shivering huddle.

After more time she drifted up from a semi-sleep to hear another sound at the door. Was it the next day, then, and time for more bread?

Dhé! The door was opening, when Mac Cailein Mor had ordered against it! Was he back, then? She shrank against the wall as an oblong of gray spread like a shaft of light into the thick black of the cell.

"Sheena?"

It was Ewen Cameron! She knew the voice of him!

"Sheena, are you awake?"

With a small gasp, Kelpie was at the door. "Och, it's near dead I am! Will you no let me free? You wouldn't see me burned, an innocent wee lass, and put to torment before it? I'll—"

"Hist!" There was a hint of strain in his voice, with a thread of humor around it. "And what were you thinking I came for? 'Tis quite likely you *are* a witch," he added ruefully, "but for all that, I cannot abide cruelty. Come away, then, and like a mouse."

Gasping with relief, Kelpie was out of the door before he had finished speaking. He groped to find her face in the dark that was to her almost light. "Wait, now. I must be bolting the door again. I cannot see."

Kelpie moved beside him and helped. "Follow me," he said when it was done. "I can put you outside the walls, and then 'tis up to you."

It was all she asked. Scarcely able to believe her good fortune, she followed him through a dark, narrow labyrinth of stone corridors, most of them damp with being underground. Twice he unlocked doors for them to pass through, and finally they crept on hands and knees through a tunnel quite as black as her cell had been. It twisted on and on, and finally upward.

" 'Tis an escape route in case of siege by an enemy,"

Ewen explained over his shoulder. "None but the family is supposed to know of it, and even they have nearly forgotten it, because for the last hundred years Clan Campbell has been too strong to be attacked in its own stronghold. Instead, it is they who attack other clans."

The narrow tunnel picked up the faint note of anger in his voice, magnified and echoed it. Kelpie, engrossed though she was in her own important affairs, suddenly wondered how it felt to be fostered by a wicked uncle who was, in addition, enemy to one's own clan, and to know you were being used as a hostage to control the actions of your own grandfather, your own people. It was the first time Kelpie had seriously tried to put herself into the mind of another person, and it felt most peculiar and disturbing.

"What if real war is coming to the Highlands?" she demanded. "Will Lochiel dare call out the Camerons to fight against your uncle and the Covenant, or—"

There was a brief silence in which their small scufflings seemed to shout aloud. Then: "Grandfather will dare to do what is right," said Ewen tersely.

Another silence, and then his low voice reached back to her again, strongly earnest. "There are things more important than safety, Sheena. I wonder if you know about them. Was it for a principle you were wanting to put a hex on my uncle, or for something else?"

Kelpie didn't answer this, for the simple reason that she

was not at all sure what a principle was. Unless— Could
it have anything to do with not using the *sgian dhu* on
herself when it seemed much easier to do so? Or had she
not used it because the thing inside her had known that
she was going to be rescued? Och, it was much too confusing to bother with now, for she could at last see a pale
blob of night sky ahead.

They emerged in a shallow cave on the hill above Inverary, not far from where Kelpie had first looked down
upon the castle.

"Now," said Ewen, "be away out of Campbell territory
as quickly as ever you can! Away around the tip of Loch
Fyne, and then east is best, but be canny. You'll not be
safe with the MacFarlanes, either, but the Stewarts of
Balquidder are hostile to the Campbell, and the Mac-
Gregors and MacNabs, and they are past Loch Lomond.
Best to skulk low during the day, for you'll not get so far
this night—though I'm hoping you'll not be found missing
until Uncle Archibald is returned and the cell door
opened."

Kelpie nodded. The weight of horror was lifting (though
she would never quite forget it), and she began to feel
quite cocky again. Fine she was now, for who knew more
about skulking and wariness in the hills? And yet through
her cockiness crept an odd curiosity.

"Will *he* be finding out 'twas you who freed me?"

"I think not," said Ewen, and there was laughter in the

lilt of his voice. "No one is thinking I know about the
secret tunnel, and they will probably believe you escaped
by witchcraft. Be careful, Sheena, the next time you're
wanting to hex someone," he added and vanished back
into the tunnel.

Kelpie stared down the blackness after him and shook
her head wonderingly. He was another daft one, to take
a risk for someone else, and with no profit to himself whatever! But she was grateful, for all that. She owed much
to his daftness.

She left the cave, lifted her face to the infinite space
of the open sky, and breathed deeply of the free air. The
moonlit side of the hill was ghostlike, a pale glow without
depth. The dark side was a soft, deep purple-black. Patches
of glimmering mist rose from the loch, and there was a
line of it behind the western hills. Kelpie laughed aloud
and headed northeast.

Thick gray mist poured over the hills from the west,
covering the world with a layer of wetness. A curlew gave
its eerie call, the whaups shrilled, and presently it began
to rain. Kelpie shivered a little, even though the gray
wool dress was the warmest she had ever owned. She
had got soft, then, living in houses. She must steal a plaidie
somewhere—preferably one of plain color, or a black and
white shepherd's tartan. Wearing the tartan of a clan
could get her into trouble.

By the time it was really light, she had passed the tip of Loch Fyne. She rested for a while, but it was cold sitting still, she was getting more and more hungry, and as there was little enough chance of being seen through the thickness of the mist she went on again. Once out of Campbell country she might risk stealing as well as begging, but she must be careful about telling fortunes or selling charms, for she would be getting near the Lowlands, where the arm of the Kirk was long and strong and people were narrow-minded about such activities. And Kelpie very much wanted to avoid any more trouble of that sort.

She waded through the dripping tangle of heather and bracken and wondered what to do next. She was free of Mina and Bogle—unless they found her again. Did she dare return to Glenfern, having left the way she had? No, for they no longer trusted her, and Alex was now her enemy. Moreover, if Mina ever found out, she would put a curse on Wee Mairi. It seemed she must give up her hopes of learning witchcraft from Mina, and any other witches who still lived in Covenant territory would be very canny and quiet indeed. She might try the Highlands, but there was a problem too, for in order to get there without re-crossing Campbell territory, she must go far east and then north and through another danger zone, where there had been fighting and trouble since spring. And even in the Highlands there was danger of meeting Mina and Bogle, and further danger that Alex might have set all the Camerons and MacDonalds against her, as he had threatened.

Dhé! Indeed and it was a braw mess she had got herself into! She cursed the Lowlander, Mina, Bogle, Mac Cailein Mor, the Kirk, and Alex, with fine impartial vigor and in two languages. Then, for good measure, she added Antrim (for forcing her hand too soon), the King (for his general fecklessness), all religious bodies, God, the Devil, and people in general.

When she had finished she felt no better, either mentally or physically. She had now traveled some twenty miles over thickly brushed and wooded hills, on an empty stomach, after a shattering experience, and even Kelpie's wiry toughness had its limits. Had she reached friendly territory yet? How was she to know without seeing a clan tartan that would tell her? Well, surely she was for the moment way ahead of any possible alarm out for her. She must have food, and there was a shieling hut below.

She sat down in the drenched heather and absently regarded a small twig of ling, already in bloom a month ahead of the ordinary heather. The tiny lantern-shaped blossoms were larger and pinker than heather too, not quite as charming, perhaps, but still tiny perfect things. Plants were nicer than people, if less exciting. She stared at it while she thought up two stories; one to use on a Campbell or a MacFarlane, the other for Stewart or MacNab. Then she stood up, brushed the wet from her skirts, and started slowly down the hill.

An old woman stepped out of the low hut to empty a pail of water, and there was no mistaking the light and dark reds crossed with green on her plaidie. It was MacNab. Her husband, no doubt, would be out in the hills with the sheep or cattle. Fine, that. Women living alone in the hills were rather more likely to be sympathetic and motherly toward a forlorn wee lass than men. (On the other hand, women of the Kirk towns were like to be dourly suspicious and hating.)

The old woman started to go back inside and then caught a glimpse of Kelpie, who stumbled a bit because she was hungry and tired—and because it was her general policy.

"Whoever is it, then?" The Highland lilt of the Gaelic was less marked here, near the Lowlands, and the voice cracked slightly with age—and yet there was in it a note like a bell.

"Och, forgive me, just." Kelpie's voice was faint, and she swayed slightly. "I am weary and hungry, and could you be sparing just a crust?"

"*Seadh*, the little love!" Mrs. MacNab was all sympathy. "Come away in, then, and I've a fine pot of oatmeal on the fire. Whatever will you be doing all alone and in the hills?" She looked at Kelpie with wise old eyes as they entered the dark shieling, and frowned in puzzlement. "From your dress you would be a lass from a Covenant home, but your face is giving it the lie."

Kelpie instantly revised her story in the brief time it took to step through the low doorway under its bristling roof of rye thatch. She stood meekly on the earthen floor under the smoke-blackened rafters and noted at a glance that these folk were better off than some, for there was a real bedstead in the corner instead of a pile of heather and bracken, and four three-legged creepie-stools.

"Eat now," invited her hostess, handing her a big bowl of oatmeal from the iron pot over the fire. "And there are bannocks here, and milk. And then perhaps you will tell me about yourself, little one, for I confess I've a fine curiosity, and strangers are none so common here."

Kelpie made use of the respite to ask some questions and get her bearings, in between ravenous mouthfuls of food. "Be ye Covenant here?" she ventured around half a bannock.

"Och, and can you no see my tartan?" demanded Mrs. MacNab. "We MacNabs are loyal to our own Stewart King, foolish darling. Why, then, are you of the Kirk?"

Kelpie shook her head vigorously. "Not I! 'Tis a prisoner of the Campbells I've been. They wanted me to be of the Covenant and refused to tell me who my parents are, at all. And so I have run away—"

"*Dhé!*" interrupted Mrs. MacNab with wide eyes. This was the most exciting thing that had happened in the braes of Balquidder this many a year. She was ready to believe anything of the hated Campbells. "Oh, my dear!

Is it that they were stealing you, then? Tell me all about it, heart's love, every bit!"

And so, replete and comfortable, warm and very nearly dry, Kelpie spun a wonderful long tale of truth and fiction mixed. The lonely old woman eagerly drank it in, with exclamations of indignation and sympathy. When Callum MacNab, looking like a twisted and weatherworn pine, came in at dusk, he had to hear it all over again, and by this time Kelpie had thought up a few more interesting details. She fairly basked in their attention and tenderness, while the old couple glowed with kindness and the rare treat of company and news. And so, with one thing and another, Kelpie spent the night and the next day with them.

12. Meeting at Pitlochry

" 'T IS sorry I am to see you away, wee dark love, but you must be putting more distance between yourself and the Campbells. And you must be searching for your own true family. To think of it! And you say Mac Cailein Mor was telling you himself that 'twas from a chief he stole you?"

"And I but a bairn," agreed Kelpie firmly. Having Callum and Alsoon believe her tale so readily almost made her believe it herself—and, after all, might not some of it be true? She tucked the little bundle of oatmeal and scones into her belt, and hugged the rough warmth of her new plaidie about her shoulders, pleased that it was the neutral black and white of the shepherd's tartan and would not associate her with any particular clan.

Luck was with her again, she reflected, that she had found these kind and simple people, willing to give her the food from their mouths and the clothes from their backs—much simpler, if less exciting, than stealing. It made her feel odd to be *given* things this way. Perhaps if all folk were like these, or like Ian and his family, there would be no need to steal. Warm with a novel sense of gratitude, she was careful not to take anything from Callum and Alsoon that they had not given her.

They stood just outside the low doorway in the brightness of the summer evening. The rain had become mere clouds glowing to the northwest, where the sun would soon dip briefly below the hills. The old couple regarded her anxiously, not at all happy to see her set off in the white gloaming.

"Look you, now," repeated Callum, "you must be going south and east for a bit, through Drummond and Stewart country, and then north through Murrays and Menzies, and when you reach Pitlochry, just be finding the home of my daughter Meg, at the tanning shop next the Tey River, and tell them I sent you, and they will care for you until you are away again."

"Aye, then," mumured Kelpie, anxious to be gone. She had heard these directions at least twice before, and in any case she knew the country far better than she dared to let Callum know.

"Haste ye back," they said, and this Highland phrase was never used unless truly meant. No one had ever said it to Kelpie before. She caught her breath, turned her head away, and hurried off.

Traveling, she found, was easier without Mina and Bogle than with them, in one way. For folks had only to take one look at those two to know the worst. But Kelpie, as long as she kept her eyes lowered and her lip tucked demurely in, looked quite innocent, so that, even on the edge of the thrifty and Kirk-trained Lowlands, people were usually willing to give her food—and when they didn't, Kelpie simply helped herself.

Now and then she picked up rumors about what was going on in the Highlands, particularly concerning Argyll, who was, it appeared, still away in the west, chasing an elusive Antrim.

As nearly as Kelpie could make out from bits here and there, Argyll had chased Antrim back to Ardnamurchen, where the latter had left his ships. But the ships had been spirited away by the English, just as Lorne had suggested, and since then the two forces had been playing catch-me-if-you-can all over the Highlands, with Antrim trying to rouse the clans against Argyll, the clans either afraid or quarreling among themselves, while Argyll tried to catch Antrim's small army before it should become a larger army.

"Aye," said an old man, chuckling, in a voice not meant to be overheard. "Argyll will never be fighting a battle against more than half his number if he can avoid it."

"Dinna mock him!" whispered another. "Ye'll no be wanting yon wild foreign Hielanders crossing the mountains wi' their wicked screechin' pipes and attacking us, will ye?"

"Dinna fret, they'll no come. 'Tis too busy they are wi' their own heathen fighting; Papists, the lot o' them."

"They might, if Montrose could stir them up tae fight for the King against the Covenant."

"They would never do that. He's a Graham from the East Coast, and those savages in the West would never stir a foot for any but their own chiefs. Anyway, they say Montrose is vanished altogether, and no doubt dead."

They both bent lowering gray brows when they saw the shamelessly eavesdropping Kelpie. She scurried away hastily, lest they think her a spy.

She wandered on, begging, stealing, and listening, until she came at last to Pitlochry.

There seemed a braw lot of people in the narrow streets of the town, and, surprisingly, many of them seemed to be wearing Gordon or MacDonald tartans. Whatever were those clans doing here? And those two young men striding along the street toward her . . . *"Dhé"* said Kelpie, and they all stopped short.

They stared at one another with mixed feelings. "Why, whatever will ye be doing here, at all?" demanded Kelpie with astonishment.

Alex recovered his wits first. "Why," he said with the old mocking grin, "we were missing you and your bonnie friends so badly that we had to come away to look for ye."

"Sssss!" remarked Kelpie, concealing her pleasure at the old bantering and reminding herself that Alex was a treacherous enemy. Moreover, she was never again going to permit herself the dangerous luxury of caring for anyone at all. Having told herself this, she turned to look at Ian with delight. A braw lad! Did he carry a grudge against her? she wondered anxiously.

"And are you all right, Kelpie?" he asked kindly. "Mina and Bogle are treating you well?"

"Sssss," she said again. "They are wicked *uruisgean,* and I have left them this long time ago. I did not want to be leaving Glenfern whatever," she added hopefully.

Ian looked pleased, but Alex laughed. "Aye, it was a good enough life you were leading there, after all. But you seem to be doing well enough for yourself the now. Where were you stealing the gey sober gown and plaidie?"

"I was not stealing them whatever!" Kelpie was outraged more by his manner than by his words.

"But you would be saying the same thing even if you had," encouraged Alex with a straight face.

Kelpie's lips began to curve upward as she remembered the teasing at the lochside at Glenfern. She tried to frown, for it was not right to be teasing with Alex when they were no longer friends. But she could not help it. "Of course," she agreed cheekily and grinned.

"Och, the wicked wee lass!" Alex chuckled. "She'll never change!"

"No, now, but she has changed!" Ian objected. "She could not laugh at herself when first she came to Glenfern."

"Are you sure 'tis herself she's laughing at?" gibed Alex. "Or is it ourselves, just, for being ready to forgive her so easily—and after she was breaking the ancient code of hospitality."

"It was not my fault!" protested Kelpie. "Mina was threatening to put a curse on you all if I did not come with them."

"Och, how tender you are of our welfare!" said Alex derisively. "And that, I suppose, is why you were so quick to tell her all about how Ian and I met the King and Montrose in Oxford?"

There was no use trying to explain, for he would never believe her—not that she cared a groat what Alex Mac-Donald thought, anyway. Perhaps she would be able to tell Ian about it some day, with Alex not around. An idea was growing in her mind. After glowering at Alex, she turned to Ian and looked up at him meltingly through long lashes. She had never before set out to beguile a lad, but Janet had put the thought in her head, and she might as well try now and see could she do it. Some deep instinct awoke, so that she seemed to know just how to go about it. "And what is it you are doing so far from Glenfern?" she asked softly.

Was it her fancy that Ian's smile seemed a wee bit

warmer than usual? "Why," he said, "we are with Colkitto's army, up at Blair Atholl, and—"

Kelpie forgot about beguiling him. "Colkitto!" she
yelped. "You mean Antrim?"

"Aye, 'tis what we call him; Alistair MacDonald, Earl
of Antrim, who has—"

"Fine I know that!" interrupted Kelpie. "But where will
Mac Cailein Mor be, then? On your tail?" There was alarm
in her voice, and both lads regarded her curiously.

"Na, na," Ian said soothingly. "He's away back to his
own country, raising a larger army, no doubt, since some
five hundred Gordons have joined us. Are you afraid of
him, Kelpie? And what are you doing here, and where are
you living?"

Kelpie looked wistful. "I am all alone, and nowhere to
live." She sighed and then smiled up at him brightly. "It
is in my mind to come along with you," she announced.

Alex laughed. Unprincipled little thing though she was,
he did enjoy her shameless, incorrigible audacity! The
workings of her mind fascinated him, and even though he
could see through her so easily, he could never remain
angry for long.

Ian looked thoughtful. "Well, and why not? We've
nearly as many women and bairns as we have men, for
Colkitto brought the whole of his clan over with him to
take back their land from the Campbells. And Lachlan
brought his wife Maeve along to be cooking and nursing

and caring for us, for she does not trust Lachlan to do it properly. You'd be far safer than wandering alone. What about it, Alex?"

Alex shrugged and lifted a red eyebrow. "Ou, I've no doubt at all that she can look after herself," he observed dryly. "But I've no objection; only, Ian *avic*, let us not be trusting her as far as tomorrow, for there is no loyalty in her."

The lazy mockery of his voice had a whiplash in it, and Kelpie flinched, unexpectedly hurt by it. She lashed back, remembering the scene in Loch nan Eilean.

"You!" she fumed. "You, to be talking of loyalty, who would strike down a friend from behind!"

Alex gaped. It was the first time she had ever caught him out of countenance, and it gave her great satisfaction. Ian looked distressed. "Och, now!" he protested hastily. "Let you both be saving your fighting for the Covenant armies. Come away back to the camp, now, and we'll talk as we go."

They started back, out of Pitlochry and over the narrow road lined with tall blooming thistles. The heather, just preparing to bloom, glowed rustily under the patchy sunlight. Alex strode along frowning, still smarting and dumfounded over the outrageous flank attack. What could she have meant by it, the wee witch? She had seemed genuinely indignant, too. For once she was not acting; Alex had been matching wits with her long enough to be sure of that. Then what under the great heavens could he have done to draw such a denunciation, such withering scorn from an unprincipled gypsy lass who would doubtless betray her own grandmother for a bit of copper? It made no sense whatever. And although Alex reminded himself that the opinion of a wee witch could scarcely matter, he found that it rankled. "*Dhiaoul!*" he muttered under his breath and knit his brows in annoyance, leaving most of the conversation to Ian.

"And why is it you're so concerned over Mac Cailein Mor, Kelpie?" Ian asked. "Have you been studying more politics since you left Glenfern?"

Kelpie hedged. "Is it likely I'd be wanting to run into the head of the Covenant army, and him death on gypsies and all who do not belong to the Kirk? No, now"—she shifted the subject—"tell me what has been happening, and why Colkitto has his army at Blair Atholl."

"Well, so." Ian thought for a minute, his sensitive profile clear and grave against the mauve and russet and olive of the August hills. Kelpie tilted her own face to look at him as she kept easy pace while Alex walked, brooding silently, behind.

"Did you know," began Ian, "that Colkitto brought over his whole clan to fight for the King against Argyll and the Covenant, and perhaps take back some of the MacDonald land from the Campbells?"

"Fine, that!" murmured Kelpie, remembering that day at Inverary. "And Argyll away after him all over the Highlands."

Ian nodded. "And the English burned Antrim's ships, so that he must stay here, will he, nil he. So he has been trying to get the other Highland clans to join him. He's not had much luck, for some of the clans fear the Campbells too much, and some others have decided that they hate the MacDonalds even more than the Covenant—for the moment, at any rate. Lochiel doesn't dare call out our clan yet, with Ewen still in Argyll's hands, and—more important—with Argyll's army so near to Lochaber. Can you imagine what would be happening to our women and children at Lochaber if Lochiel took the men away to fight the Covenant?"

Kelpie could imagine, easily. Her blood ran cold at the thought of Wee Mairi in danger, and she nodded soberly.

"Some of us Camerons have come along anyway, and so have some five hundred Gordons who are wanting revenge against Argyll," continued Ian. "But most on this side of the mountains think we Western Highlanders are a band of wild savages, like the Red Indians of America. And even Stewart of Atholl—although he hates Argyll and the Covenant—will have nothing to do with the Irish MacDonalds. So—" He grinned at Kelpie mischievously. "We have just borrowed Atholl's castle from him, and now we sit

and wait." He sobered again. "I do not know what we will
do next. There is a rumor that Graham of Montrose is still
alive, and perhaps he is our hope. But to tell the truth,
things do not look very good, and the Covenant armies
will not sit still forever."

Kelpie's lip lifted in sudden anger. "Och, ye will be
losing this war, just!" she predicted despairingly. "For
yourselves, and for the folk like me who want only to be
left alone. You cannot get together even to save your own
lives, but must always be quarreling clan against clan, and
so ye will lose!"

Ian looked depressed, but Alex came out of his black
reverie with a laugh. "Listen to her, just!" he taunted. "The
lone lass who lives for herself and no other will be giving
us a lesson on cooperation! But even though you don't
practice what you preach," he added somberly, "you're
right."

A puffy cloud blew over the sun, darkening the bright
hills, and the thistles waved in a sudden sharp breeze.

The small army was spread over the hill and moor near
Blair Atholl, looking somewhat dispirited. Some men were
hopefully cleaning their gear, polishing the huge two-
handed claymores and battle axes which struck such terror
into Lowland hearts. Others just sat, or wandered, or gam-
bled, or talked. Women were busy gossiping, sewing, cook-

ing, arguing; but one tall, gaunt woman brooded alone. Children ran about playing tag or hanging about the men. A ragged, motley crowd it was, but fierce-looking enough, no doubt, to folk on this side of the mountains. Kelpie frowned suddenly. The whole scene looked familiar.

"We've set up our wee camp spot over yon, just near those rowan trees," said Ian, pointing to a spot partway up the hill. But before they were halfway there a flurry of excitement near the edge of the moor turned into an uproar. Men began shouting, running. A single shot was fired, and then several more.

"It couldn't be an attack!" Ian frowned, staring across the moor, "but what is it?"

"'Tis he!" shouted Alex. "'Tis Graham of Montrose! Look you there!"

"The King's Lieutenant!" "He's come!" "My Lord of Montrose!" The words were being shouted back and forth, and the sound swelled into a thunder of cheers. Kelpie found herself running with the lads toward the center of the excitement.

As nearly as she could see through the crowd, the Lord of Montrose seemed to be a slight young man in groom's clothing, with brown hair and a bunch of oats stuck in his bonnet. *Dhé!* She had seen him before! And now from the wooded hill a red-bearded giant in the MacDonald tartan —Antrim—rushed down to clasp the hand of the slight young man, and Kelpie remembered. She had seen it in the crystal, that first morning at Glenfern.

And so now they had come together, Antrim and Montrose, totally different and yet fighting for the King's cause. What would be the outcome?

13. The Hexing of Alex

THE immediate effect of Montrose's arrival was that of a most powerful magic charm. It could not have been more telling had he come with a full army at his back instead of just one man, his cousin Patrick. The King's standard was raised then and there on the hillside and saluted with a flourish of trumpets, and cheers, and triumphantly skirling bagpipes. And some of the clans who had been hovering about waiting to attack the Irish Highlander Antrim now came to join the King's Lieutenant, Montrose—including Stewart of Atholl.

Kelpie decided to stay for a while. Things looked interesting. She was safer here than wandering alone. Besides, she liked Ian's company, even if it meant putting up with Alex. She even thought that she just might persuade Ian to guard himself against his precious foster brother, though she had not much hope of this, Ian being so stubbornly trustful. Besides, since she had "seen" the thing in the loch, it would surely happen, and there was nothing she could do to stop it.

For a while, staying with the army meant simply staying right there where it was. Nothing much seemed to be happening. Clans—or, more often, bits of them—drifted in. Kelpie roamed where she liked, usually with the lads and their watchful *ghillie,* Lachlan, exchanging insults with Alex and hostile silence with Lachlan and his wife Maeve, who had no use for her whatever and made no secret of it.

She also spent some of her time gazing speculatively at the tall, gaunt woman whom she had noticed the first day she arrived. The woman would stare for hours into space, a black, brooding look on her face, her hands twisting together as if she were wringing someone's neck —or perhaps casting a new kind of spell. A bulky Gordon plaidie covered her broad shoulders, and, though she was not old, there was the beginning of gray at her dark temples, and there were strong, grim lines along her mouth. Her eyes were deep-set and a little alarming, and Kelpie wondered whether she might be a witch. She looked it. Perhaps she had been tortured by witch-hunters and had somehow escaped? Kelpie considered approaching her about learning the Evil Eye, but the woman's fierceness made her hesitate. She might get a curse put on herself for her boldness, and she could do fine without *that.*

The coppery hills began to turn purple with the blooming of the heather. It rained. No more was heard of Argyll, but there were rumors that the enemy commander, Lord Elcho, was in Perth with an army of seven thousand and looking with considerable interest toward Blair Atholl. "And we with only two thousand men," commented Alex cheerfully.

"Ou, aye," agreed Ian with a grin. "But just think of our fine store of weapons!" Lachlan looked sour, and Kelpie raised a derisive eyebrow.

"Artillery?" mused Alex. "None."

"Cavalry—three old horses, one of them lame," chanted Ian.

"Guns—some old-fashioned matchlocks, and all the ammunition we could be needing to shoot a third of them for one round each."

"And then," finished Ian in triumph, "just in case we're needing them, there's a few swords, claymores, and battle-axes—not to mention the *sgian dhu*," he added, reaching down to tap the wee dirk where it nestled in his stocking, just on the outside of his right knee.

"And"—Alex chuckled with ironic optimism—"Montrose has been saying that the enemy has plenty of weapons, and those of us without can just help ourselves once the fighting has started."

Kelpie looked at them. There was, she felt, a definite limit to the things a body should be joking about. She said so. And Lachlan, who felt personally responsible for the safety of Ian and Alex, for once agreed with her.

And now came Maeve, whose loyalty was all toward Mac 'ic Ian, heir to Glenfern (for Master Alex, although a foster son, was not actually a Cameron at all). Her orange hair gleamed even in the cloud-filtered sun, and she addressed herself to Ian.

"Food will be ready," she said and crossed herself as she looked at Kelpie. As they all started toward the rowan tree they called home, she added, half under her breath, "Herself eats enough, whatever, but will never be doing any cooking."

"You were not liking my cooking," observed Kelpie complacently. It was no accident that the one meal she had produced, at Alex' insistence, had been perfectly awful.

"*Dhé,* no!" Ian agreed, laughing. "You said she was trying to poison us, Maeve. You'd not be wanting to try that again, would you?"

" 'Tis gey queer," retorted Maeve, "for a gypsy not to be able to cook over an open fire."

Ian looked at Kelpie, his keen mind as usual fighting with his desire to believe the best of people. Alex began to laugh. "Och!" he exclaimed ruefully. "And I the one who was never going to be fooled by her again!"

Kelpie saw an opening. "Gypsy taste will be different from yours," she announced blandly. "When I was first stolen, it was a dreadful time I had getting used to gypsy food! It was nearly starving I was, for a while." Her blue ringed eyes widened with the picture of a poor wee bairn pining away with hunger.

Lachlan snorted.

"Ou, the pity of it!" said Alex mournfully, his angular face looking almost tender. "And you used to royal food, and all. I've wondered, just, whether 'tis yourself was the princess stolen from our King and Queen all those long years ago when they visited the Highlands."

For a minute Kelpie was fooled. Her eyes were a smoky blue blaze as visions of royal grandeur hurtled through her mind. Of course! Why not?

"For shame, Alex," said Ian reproachfully. "She's nearly believing it."

Kelpie jerked out of her dream and hissed venomously at Alex, who chuckled impenitently and wondered how she would try to get even this time.

The next day Kelpie went down to the burn, where she had noticed that the soil had a sticky, claylike quality. There she sat for some time, screened by broom and high bracken, and slowly shaped a small clay figure—not that it looked much like Alex, she being no artist. In fact, she admitted, a body could barely tell that it was supposed to be human at all. But perhaps the intent was the main thing. If only she could get hold of a bit of his hair or a fingernail—but Kelpie had had enough of hair-stealing for a while, particularly red hair. Anyway, Alex was much too canny. She had never yet managed to steal anything from him without being caught. No, she would just have to be trying her hex without it.

There were brambles conveniently near. Kelpie picked a long thorn, regarded her clay figure thoughtfully, and then plunged the thorn deep into the area where the stomach might be expected to be.

Then she wrapped up the hex figure, went back to the rowan tree, and began to watch Alex hopefully.

Two days passed, but if he had any pains in his stomach, he concealed them very well. Kelpie added a second thorn to the figure, this time in the head, and again waited. By rights, his brains ought to start melting away, but she must not be doing it right, for Alex's brains remained as uncomfortably keen as ever. He didn't even get a headache.

Kelpie began looking wistfully at the tall, gaunt woman again. If she *was* a witch, she could undoubtedly help. And yet—Kelpie noticed that the men of the army did not treat her at all as a witch. Far from shunning her, they went out of their way to be kind, to bring her choice bits of food, to talk to her. Once again Kelpie decided not to risk trouble. She would manage her own hex, impotent as it seemed to be.

In disgust, she took it out again, plunged thorns all over it, rubbed it with nettles, burned it, and then watched again. After five days Alex did twist his wrist slightly, but somehow Kelpie failed to feel much satisfaction. She was quite sure that she had never put a thorn in the left wrist. So she gave up trying to hex him. Either she didn't have the power at all, or else—which seemed quite possible— Alex had a greater power.

Lord Graham of Montrose had a great power too. Kelpie found herself more and more interested in him. The look of him was not that of a strong leader at all. Slight, he was, with gentle dark gray eyes and a quiet and courteous air that hardly seemed to belong in an army at all, much less at the head of one. Now, Antrim looked like a leader indeed, massive red giant that he was, with a great roar of a voice. Yet there was no doubt that Montrose was the heart and soul of the army. Everyone, even Antrim, listened to him with respect amounting almost to worship, and everyone said that he had a genius for warfare.

Was it magic? Quite likely, Kelpie thought. She took to watching and listening whenever he was among the men. But she never saw him make any magic signs, and his words were about such things as honor and loyalty and why he was fighting for the King. Ian had said Montrose wanted no power for himself, but only for right to be done, but Ian was gullible. Skeptical, Kelpie kept her ears open.

"Loyalty is the great thing," Montrose remarked one day, sitting at ease in a misty drizzle, kilted Highlanders all around him. They listened with eagerness and respect, but Kelpie, at the edge of the group, narrowed her eyes mistrustfully.

"Loyalty to your clan and your King, to an ideal, to a friend, to a thing you believe," he went on. "This is integrity; and it is loyalty also to yourself." Kelpie frowned. It was only loyalty to oneself that paid. She had found that out. Montrose was like Ian, then, too generous and trusting. They would both suffer for it, no doubt, unless they learned to care only for their own welfare.

"You see," said Montrose, "King Charles is a Stewart, and so we have a double loyalty to him—as our King, and as a Stewart and a Highlander. The English Parliament and the Scottish Covenant wish to rule the King and all of us as well. I think I need not tell you that."

There was a growl from the group. "Aye, Mac Cailein Mor would be King Campbell with the help of the Covenanters!" "A plague on the lot of them!"

"And so," urged Montrose, "we must put aside lesser loyalties and quarrels amongst our own clans, and stand together."

"Aye!" shouted the men, but Kelpie privately thought that Montrose's magic would fail at this point. Who ever knew a Highlander to give up his clan feuds for anything at all—except a greater clan feud?

She did learn one thing about Montrose. He used different words with different kinds of people—just as she herself did, in a way. She was eavesdropping one evening as he sat by his campfire with Antrim and Patrick Graham of Inchbrakie, and his words to them were less simple and certain than those to the untaught clansmen.

"No," he said, "I do not fight for what people call the Divine Right of Kings. I don't believe there is such a thing, Alistair. A king must be subject to the laws of God, nature, and the country that he rules. But as long as he stays within those laws, then he should *be* the ruler."

"And if he doesn't?" It was Patrick Graham, called "Black Pate."

The youthful face looked troubled in the firelight. "It's true King Charles hasn't always obeyed the rules," murmured Montrose. "That is why I supported the Covenant at first. But then I saw the greater danger we courted. If a group of subjects takes over the king's power, they may become a far worse tyrant than ever a king could be, and that is what happened. You see yourselves how the Covenant oppresses the people; and I think those who are fighting for the Parliament in this war may find that they've used their own blood and their own fortunes to buy vultures and tigers to rule over them. To tell you the truth, my friends, I don't know the right way to handle a king who abuses his power, but I do know that this is the wrong way. Perhaps there should be some limit set to the amount of power that one man or group can have."

Kelpie chewed her lip thoughtfully. Och, now, and there was a good idea. She could think of several such

whose power should be limited to nothing at all. She
would begin with Argyll and the Covenant, and go on to
the Lowlander and Mina and Bogle. But how would one
set about arranging this?

In her preoccupation, Kelpie forgot that she was hiding
and carelessly shifted her position so that a twig cracked.
A small twig it was, and most folk would never have
noticed, but these men were well schooled in danger.
Three heads turned as one, and an instant later Antrim's
huge hand was plucking her from her hiding place as he
would a puppy.

"*Dhé!*" He chortled, holding her up in the orange light
of the fire and looking her over with interest. "Here's a
fine dangerous enemy in our midst."

"Och, indeed and I am not!" protested Kelpie as well
as she could. She tucked in her lip and looked pathetically
at Montrose. "Do not be letting him hurt me, your Lordship!" she begged in English. " 'Tis only a poor, wee, harmless—"

"Let her down, Alistair," suggested Montrose gently,
"and perhaps she can tell us what she was doing there."

"Spying for Argyll, perhaps?" suggested Patrick nar-
rowly, looking at her gray dress.

Kelpie's indignation was genuine. "That *nathrach!*" She
sputtered earnestly and went on to curse him vigorously.
"He is a *droch-inntinneach uruisg* and a redhaired devil
with a black heart in him!"

Montrose, who knew little Gaelic, looked interested. "What was that?" he inquired, and Antrim chuckled.

"She called him a serpent and an evil-minded monster," he translated. "And I'm thinking she meant it, too! Well, then, why *were* you skulking there, lass?"

Once again Kelpie found semi-truth to be the most effective answer. "Och," she whispered, ducking her head shyly. "I was wanting to see himself, and to be hearing him talk, for the singing tongue in his mouth." From beneath lowered lids she observed that their faces were amused and tolerant.

"Well, and so you've heard him," said Antrim, not un-kindly. "Away with you, then, and don't be doing it again. Next time you might just be getting a claymore instead of a question."

Kelpie left meekly enough, relieved to get off so easily. But none of her questions was really answered. She had wanted to learn the source of Montrose's power, and whether or no it was from magic, and if and how she could learn it. For although it was just possible that Mont-rose could destroy his archenemy, Argyll, which would be a fine thing indeed, Kelpie felt that Mina and Bogle and the Lowlander were another matter, and up to her. For sooner or later she was almost sure to run into them again, and when that day came she was going to need a great deal of magic power indeed!

14. The Battle of Tippermuir

A<small>T LAST</small> word went round that the army was to move,
but not, as Kelpie had expected, away from the danger of Perth and Lord Elcho's great army. Quite the contrary. They were, it seemed, going to take Perth.

Recklessness and practical caution fought within Kelpie. A fine, daft, gallant, and suicidal idea it seemed to her. If she had any sense in the head of her, she would take her leave now and head for safety. But she decided, instead, to go along but to stay with the women and children well behind the lines, once the fighting started, and then take to the hills when the battle was lost.

The small, poorly equipped army gathered itself together and started south to the sound of pipes playing valiantly. They had got no farther than the hill of Buchanty when they ran into one of the enemy forces which had been surrounding them all the time. A full five hundred bowmen it must be, and Kelpie looked around hastily for something to hide under.

But she had reckoned without Montrose. He and Antrim rode to meet the two leaders of the bowmen, and they talked. And, sometime during the talking, Montrose cast his spell, for presently the two forces spread out over the purple masses of blooming heather and ate together, the leaders still talking over wine and food.

And then one of the enemy leaders sprang to his feet, and Kelpie could hear his words clearly. "You're wrong!" he shouted. " 'Tis not two thousand men ye have, but two thousand and five hundred! For we'll never be fighting against Montrose!"

Kelpie shook her head wonderingly. Why on earth did Montrose fight at all, if he could do this? Or did Argyll and others have some kind of counter-magic? Kelpie began to feel newly discouraged about her own prospects for magical powers, with so much competition about.

The newly expanded army moved on again, undisturbed by the news that, in addition to his seven thousand infantry, Lord Elcho also had some eight hundred cavalry and nine pieces of heavy artillery. The Highlanders, like Kelpie, put their faith in the magic of Montrose. With him to lead them, no force on earth could beat them.

They spent the night on the moor of Fowlis, and early in the morning were away down the Small Glen, and on to Tippermuir. There stood the walled town of Perth, some three miles away. And between stood the Covenant army, spread wide, waiting to catch Montrose's impudent small army between its fierce jaws.

Kelpie looked at it with awe, and some of her assurance left her. Surely, now, Montrose was stretching his powers too far! Lord Elcho would be wiping them out as easily as Antrim might knock down herself. There they stood, six deep, every man protected by corselet and an iron head-piece, and the most of them armed with muskets, against one-third the number of Highlanders, who wore only rag-ged kilts and rawhide brogans and had claymores and bows and arrows, or no weapons at all. It was a sad con-trast.

The citizens of Perth seemed to regard the coming bat-tle as a fine new kind of Sabbath sport, for they had turned out in great numbers to watch the fun. Kelpie shoved through the palpitating crowd of women and children, now well behind the army, until she reached a spot on high ground which gave her both a good view and a quick escape route for when she needed it. And she ex-pected to need it. She hoped that Ian might escape the slaughter somehow, but she was going to be quite sure that *she* did.

Ian, who had an even better view in his spot in the front row of the battle line, was not feeling very optimistic himself. He looked with resignation over the flaunting blue banners of the Covenant ranks bearing the motto: *For Christ's Crown and Covenant*—and then back to the one brave royal banner—three golden leopards on a red background—floating above the Highland rabble. The breeze rippled its folds and shivered across the purpled moors. It seemed too fine a day for men to die.

Alex turned from chaffing his cousins among the small band of Keppoch MacDonalds and looked at Ian. There was a touch of pallor beneath the sunburn of his angular face, but his eyes were bright.

"And are you frightened, Ian?" he asked with a crooked grin.

"As ever was!" retorted Ian forthrightly, and Alex chuckled.

"And I too," he agreed. "My cousin Archie has just been saying it's only a fool does not fear danger—in which case, I'm a wise man indeed!"

Ian looked around him. Most of the ordinary clansmen seemed not much worried. There was an almost supernatural faith in Montrose, that he would bring victory at any odds. And Antrim—the magnificent Colkitto—strode down the line with confidence in every inch of him. His legs were pillars beneath the MacDonald kilt he wore, and they were matched by the size of his shoulders.

"I think *he* isn't afraid," observed Ian.

Alex nodded agreement. "Montrose is worried, though,"

he murmured. "You can see it behind his eyes. What is happening now?" For one of Montrose's officers was going toward Lord Elcho, waving a white flag of truce.

"Here's Ranald," said Archie. "He'll know. Ranald learns everything." If Archie was frightened, one would never know it. His black eyes sparkled wickedly from under his thick black hair, and he turned eagerly to make room for another Keppoch cousin. "What is it Ranald, *avic?*"

"An envoy of courtesy," reported Ranald, shaking his fair head wonderingly. "Montrose has sent to ask is it against their principles to fight on the Sabbath, and would they rather wait for tomorrow. Only Montrose would think to make such a gesture!"

Archie, who seemed to have a low opinion of Covenant principles, shook his head disapprovingly. Alex opened his mouth for a jesting remark, and forgot to close it again. For, incredibly, outrageously, the envoy was being taken prisoner! He was seized, bound, hustled off through the Covenant ranks.

Incredulous anger rippled through the Highland army. Ian stood aghast. "He couldn't!" he whispered. "He *couldn't* violate a flag of truce!" And for once even the more cynical Alex shared Ian's feelings.

Oddly, Kelpie's face came to Alex at that moment. Her narrow, slant-eyed, impudent face would be wondering what was so awful about violating a white flag. Was it any worse than killing a man in battle? And the envoy wasn't even dead—yet, anyway. To his disgust, Alex found himself, in his own mind, trying to explain it to her. *"Dhiaoul!"* he muttered and turned his attention to the matters at hand.

It was quite possible that Lord Elcho had done himself an ill service, for a flame of Celtic rage had engulfed the Highland army. Alex found that he had shifted forward an inch or two without knowing it, and the rest of the army with him. Those without weapons had picked up stones. For a moment it seemed that they would all break into a wild charge, but Montrose achieved the minor miracle of holding them back. "Wait!" said his outflung arm. "Wait!" boomed Antrim. "Be patient a wee while, men of my heart, and we soon will be giving them cold steel for it."

And they waited, only inching forward a toe at a time, as the Covenant army moved closer, until not a hundred paces separated them. A long wait it seemed, long enough for all the army to hear Lord Elcho's answer to the message of the unfortunate envoy. "The Lord's Day," he had said, "is fit for the Lord's work of exterminating the barbarous Irish and Highlanders."

"When we charge," muttered Archie, who had been in battles before, "keep just one thing in mind. Choose your enemy and kill him, and then a second man if you can."

"Very well so," agreed Alex mildly. "And what will I do with my third man?" He was pleased that his voice had just the nonchalance he wanted for it.

Ian's was equally cool. "Just be leaving him to me," he said. "I'll have had my three by then."

Another inch forward, and the Covenanters closer yet, and still no signal to charge. And now came the Covenant battle cry for the day. "Jesus and no quarter!" they yelled, and Ian shuddered at the blasphemy.

And then suddenly came a shrill wild skirl from the gaunt woman at the back of the battle. A voice lifted and pealed savagely. "Wolves of the North! Let the fangs bite!"

And the signal was given, and as they rushed forward Ian's voice answered with his own clan battle cry. "Sons of the dogs, come hither, come hither, and ye shall have flesh!"

"God and St. Andrew!" answered the Keppoch Mac-Donalds, and the air was thick with the wailing menace of pipes and clan cries, until the pipers abandoned their pipes for the claymores, and the slogans became scattered and mixed with mere yells.

Neither Alex nor Ian remembered the rest clearly— only a wall of armed men ahead, and then the smashing, tearing impact of battle. There was Archie's fighting laughter, and the blazing red beard of Antrim . . . some-one yelling "A Gordon, a Gordon!" the whole of the fight. And then there was no wall of armored men, but only fleeing backs, and the charge went on and on—until they were at the gates of Perth.

When Kelpie reached Perth, some time later (and a messy three miles it was too, littered with Covenant casualties), she fully expected to find it being thoroughly sacked and looted, and to be in time to pick up a few wee things herself. It was just for this that she had managed to get slightly ahead of the rest of the women and children.

But there was unexpected quiet and order. Kelpie paused inside the gate, frowning. A few citizens peered fearfully from windows, waiting for the worst, but the worst did not seem to be happening. Instead, Highlanders stood about, glaring at the frightened heads and at a shouting preacher on the near corner, and looking disgruntled.

"He shall rain snares upon the sinners," screamed the preacher, "and fire and brimstone and storms of wind shall be the portion of their cup!"

Kelpie joined a group of ragged Highlanders who were standing there listening. "*Now* will he remember their iniquity and visit their sins!" the preacher was suggesting hopefully. "I will consume them by the sword, and by the famine, and by the pestilence! I will pour their wickedness upon them!"

"Is it ourselves he means?" asked Kelpie of the nearest Highlander.

He nodded, looking disgusted. "And we not even allowed to feed his words back to him," he growled. "And," he added regretfully, "I am thinking that the fine coat of him would be fitting me, whatever."

"But why? Why not be silencing him and taking it?" demanded Kelpie. He shrugged, looking aggressive. Montrose, it seemed, had ordered no sacking, no looting, no harm to the citizens.

Several Highlanders turned from the preacher, who was now informing them that they were to be cast forth from the land, and chimed in. An unheard-of thing, that! And they half-starved and in rags, and counting on food, clothing, and a fine wee bit of loot from these overfed, psalm-singing heathen hypocrites! And what was Montrose about, then, to be depriving them of their just reward? And yet, not a man suggested disobeying.

The preacher, a gaunt, long-faced man in a fine black coat, was working himself up into a fine passion of Covenanter Christianity. "They shall die grievous deaths," he announced. "They shall not be lamented, neither shall they be buried; they shall be as dung upon the face of the earth."

"Is it his own friends he's speaking of?" came Alex's mocking voice. " 'Tis a fine burial service you're preaching, my friend, but shouldn't you be helping to dig the graves first?"

The preacher stopped, glared, and began to launch forth

with more Bible verses. But the Highlanders had got the idea.

"Now then," one of them called, chortling. " 'Twould be no harm to the bonnie man if we just see to it that he helps bury his friends, now, would it? Come away out, now, and be useful!" And in a moment the preacher was being propelled firmly out of the gate, protesting loudly that yon muckle redshanks were gang to murther him. Alex and Ian, Archie and Ranald were left, grinning after them.

Kelpie spared them no more than a glance and then returned to her grievance. No looting! And she had been wanting a nice silver belt and perhaps a silken purse.

Disgustingly, Ian and Alex agreed with Montrose. " 'Tis a barbaric practice, sacking cities," said Ian with quiet intensity. "Why should soldiers war on civilians, especially women and bairns? If there were more leaders with the principles of Montrose, war would be less evil than it is."

"There's no use one army stopping, and the others going on doing it," argued Kelpie.

"Someone must be stopping first," Alex pointed out. Odd how he kept trying to explain principles to this little witch, who could no more understand them than could his cousin Cecily's wee and wicked yellow kitten. "If Montrose shows mercy, perhaps the Covenanters will do the same."

Kelpie sneered audibly, and Archie made a rude noise.

Alex shrugged. "To be more practical," he pointed out, "perhaps Montrose is hoping that these towns near his own home may be turned to our side if we treat them well."

"I think he would do so anyway," insisted Ian, " 'Tis a point of integrity, Kelpie."

Kelpie looked blank, and Alex laughed. "Do not be trying to explain integrity to *her*, Ian!" he pleaded. "Begin first on a creature with more capacity—like Cecily's kitten, for example—and then Dubh, perhaps, and after that you might be working up to a kelpie."

At the mention of Cecily, Ian saw in his mind a heart-shaped, mischievous face in a halo of tawny hair. And then he put it away from him, for Alex had said fifty times that he was going to marry his cousin one day; and if his foster brother wanted Cecily, then she was not for Ian to think of. So he thought instead of Kelpie, who was tossing her black head scornfully.

"Well, whatever integrity is," she announced, "this is daft. For," she predicted with gloomy relish, "all the towns around will be thinking they may do as they please, with no fear of punishment. Just wait you now, they'll be shouting more loudly and burning more witches than ever before."

Surprisingly, Alex nodded. It was Ian who was about to argue. But at this moment Lachlan and Maeve arrived, shouting that at last they had found Mac 'ic Ian, and would he be coming away this minute to have his sore wound tended.

Ian laughed, faintly embarrassed, and began to protest. And Kelpie, with a pang of concern, noticed for the first time that his plaidie was wrapped oddly about his left arm and that a stain of red was creeping along the sleeve beneath it.

"*Dhé!*" she cried. "It may be only a wee bit cut as you say, Ian, but yon orange-top"—she glared at Maeve— "has not the sense to be tending it for you, and it will surely mortify if you let her. I," she announced firmly, "will bind it myself, with bread mold and cobwebs on the cut, and a wee charm or two over it, and 'twill heal overnight, for I know about such matters."

Maeve promptly screamed that the wicked little witch would poison Mac 'ic Ian only over her dead body. Kelpie retorted that it was a fine idea, that last. Ranald said that he had known mold and cobwebs to work very well. Archie's black eyes sparkled with amusement, and it fell upon Alex to arbitrate.

Firmly, with the masterful air that Kelpie usually resented hotly, he declared in favor of her bread mold but against her charms. He pacified Maeve by allowing her to supervise and to put the sign of the cross upon Ian's arm. And because both Maeve and Kelpie were genuinely concerned over Ian's welfare a truce of sorts was declared —for the moment.

15. Witch Hunt

AN UNEASY peace brooded over the whole of Perth the
next day. Not only the citizens but also their Gaelic
conquerors tended to feel slightly abused, and they spent
the morning glooming at one another. By noon the high
Celtic spirits had risen again in the conquerors, and a
spirit of mischief took over. They released prisoners from
stocks and jails (most of them guilty of such crimes as
failing to attend kirk), and some of the Irish MacDonalds
began preaching back at the dour, hell-spouting Calvinist
preachers.

But this palled too, and presently a group of young and
adventurous Highlanders decided just to go out and have
a wee look round the neighboring countryside. Archie and
Ranald came hunting Alex and Ian, who were delighted.
Lachlan firmly attached himself to the party, with strict

orders from Maeve not to be letting Mac 'ic Ian anything to start his cut bleeding afresh.

At this point Kelpie announced that she would just go too. Ranald looked at her dubiously, but Archie laughed. "And why ever not?" he demanded. "The women do full share of work, what with cooking and nursing, and should have a bit of fun when they can. Will you come too, Maeve?"

Maeve hesitated, glared at Kelpie, and declined. And the party, some dozen or fifteen altogether, set off.

"Is Kelpie your true name?" demanded Archie as they started west across the sweep of moor. He grinned at her engagingly. "It wouldn't be every day a body could have a kelpie as mascot. Tell me," he asked, "have I seen you turn a soft eye upon Ian? Could you not be giving him a wee love potion?"

Kelpie smiled enigmatically and declined to answer. But she turned the idea over in her mind.

It was a lovely day, this second of September. The birches were beginning to yellow and the bracken to turn rusty underneath. Rowan trees flaunted clumps of brilliant red-orange berries in the sun; and only now and again did a cloud shadow glide silently over the rosy-heathered swelling ground, patching it with somber purple. Kelpie tied her plaidie around her waist, for she would not be needing it until the chill of evening.

They walked on, with the long, tireless Highland stride,

chattering and laughing with the upsurge of spirits that
was a normal reaction from the fear and triumph of yesterday.

"And did you get your dozen men, Alex?" inquired the
fair-haired Ranald. I saw you once cutting down an armored musketeer twice your size, and glad I was to be
fighting with and not against you."

Alex's red brows slanted upward. "*Dhé!*" he said. "I was
so frighted I just held out my sword, and it seems the
enemy was obliging enough to run into it. 'Twas Ian was
the braw fighter, and none better in Scotland. It was he
saved me more than once."

"Only so that you could be saving me, Alex *avic,*" retorted Ian, "and Lachlan saving the both of us," he added.
"Besides, it was I was so scared I could only think to run
away."

"And since you were headed for Perth, already, the only
thing to do was just cut your way through the face of the
enemy," finished Archie with bland seriousness.

Ian nodded gravely. "That was the way of it. I was too
frightened to think of turning around."

And so they went on, with the same old bantering
Kelpie had heard so often at Glenfern, and each of them
claiming to have been more frightened than any of the
rest. Kelpie listened with an odd feeling of contentment.
This brotherhood, this easy straight-faced teasing which
was an unspoken love between friends, was a warm and

joyous thing to hear—for all that it was dangerous to have it. There was wistfulness in her heart as she walked silently among the cheerful group, and a shadow on her face.

Presently they came to a river and a small gray town on the near side. "I doubt they'll love us there," predicted a tall lad in Duncan kilt, "but perhaps their good Lowland sense of business will make them willing to sell us a pint or two of ale—or even good *uisghebaugh,* if there is such a thing outside of the Highlands."

It was a popular suggestion, and the long Highland strides became even longer, so that Kelpie—though she denied it—had to stretch her own to keep up. As they drew near the cluster of stone houses with the somber square kirk in the center, she frowned a little. A dour, gloomy place it was! Not that it looked different, really, from other towns, but there was a bad feel to it. None of the others seemed to notice, but Kelpie's bones were wary.

There seemed to be very few people about. Perhaps most of them had seen the Highlanders coming and gone inside. The few folk they did meet cast looks of hate at the kilted barbarians—which the barbarians, secure in the safety of numbers and reputation, found rather amusing.

An innkeeper sourly sold them ale, with black looks thrown in for good measure. "Och, wouldn't he like to poison it, just!" said Alex in Gaelic as Kelpie refused the ale Ian offered her. It might not actually be poisoned, but it could have an evil spell on it, all the same. She said so.

"If your spells haven't worked, I doubt anyone's could!" Alex taunted her. "For you've tried hard enough, haven't you?"

Kelpie glowered from under her thick lashes. Had he seen her, then, all that while at Blair Atholl? Or was it just his evil way of always knowing what she was thinking? She had begun to feel a trifle more friendly since learning that he had saved Ian yesterday instead of cutting him down. But once again Alex was taking the offensive.

Alex had known what she was about at Blair Atholl, and it had amused him, in a way—once he was sure her spells were impotent. But just now, for some reason, all her hatred for him was rankling, and he was in the mood to goad her a bit for her irritating ways—although he was not at all sure why she got under his skin so easily. So he deliberately treated her to his most satirical grin. "And didn't your hex work at all, poor lass?" he inquired sympathetically.

Kelpie started to hiss at him, but Ian was looking at her oddly. He would not take it kindly that she had tried to hex his foster brother, even though it was himself she was trying to protect. And she wanted to keep Ian's good will.

Her lip drooped. "Always and always you will be thinking evil of me, Alex MacDonald!" she lamented. "You will be trying to make everyone hate me, and never giving me the chance at all to be better, no matter how I might try."

The other lads were listening to all this with great interest, and they now regarded Alex with severity, and Kelpie with sympathy. But it was Ian's sympathy she wanted—and got.

" 'Tis true enough, Alex," he said accusingly. "You've ever thought the worst of the poor lass, and her only sin is in being what she was taught to be. How could she ever change with you condemning her in advance?"

A rare blaze of rage swept over Alex. *"Dhiaoul!* 'Tis a fool you are, Ian!" And suddenly he was quarreling—it was incredible—with his foster brother, dearer than kin, and over a young rogue of a gypsy lass not worth a hair on Ian's head! And yet the quarrel went on and on.

Kelpie had never seen them angry at each other before, and she was frightened. It was the town had done it! The town was filled with hate and malice and had put a spell on them all! And she, who should be pleased at seeing Ian turn from Alex, found that she couldn't enjoy it. She couldn't even bear to listen. She slipped out of the tavern with their angry words drifting after her.

The streets were no longer empty. A crowd was streaming out of the four-square meeting house and along toward the town square, and it was the sort of crowd she knew all too well. Their faces held a savage and bloodthirsty fanaticism, and this was not a mob looking for a victim, but one which had found one. It was someone, no doubt,

who had committed the sin of breaking the Sabbath, or
dancing, or perhaps chancing to glance at a neighbor's
cow before it fell ill. Och, it was a witch trial they had
been having! No knowing was it a real witch or not, nor
would it matter; for to be accused was to be condemned.

"Burn them!" the crowd growled as it surged past the
tavern. Kelpie should have ducked back inside, but her
curiosity was too great. And despite her vow to be hard-
hearted there was a flicker in her of pity. The victims were
coming now, being roughly hustled along toward the
square. The crowd swept Kelpie along, not noticing one
more gray gown among so many others.

Kelpie squeezed through a gap between a stout man
and a bony woman, and as it closed behind her she found
herself almost pushed against the victims, her eyes staring
straight into theirs—and their eyes were as filled with
hatred as those of the crowd.

Mina and Bogle!

Panic gripped her heart. Frantically she tried to back
up, to melt back into the crowd. But there was no gap
now, only a wall of townsmen at her back. And it was
too late. Mina's shrill screech cut the other sounds.

"There she is! The kelpie who led us into witchcraft!
In the gray dress! There! Look at the ringed eyes of her!"

"She'll be putting the Evil Eye on ye all" croaked Bogle
venomously.

Sick fear and revulsion were in Kelpie as her quick eyes

swept around—vainly—for an avenue of escape. They were not accusing her to save themselves, which would have been logical, but in sheer malice. That she might have done the same didn't occur to her, for there was no time for thinking. The crowd was responding with a new roar, seeking more blood, turning to find its new victim.

Kelpie looked instinctively for a scapegoat, another gray dress to point out—but again, too late. Hands grabbed her. She wrenched free with a twist, only to be grasped by more hands, caught beyond hope of escape.

"Alex!" screamed Kelpie. "Ian! Help!" And she lifted her voice in the Cameron war rant, hoping that the familiar words might reach Ian. *"Chlanna non can, thigibh a so—"* A blow on the head cut it short, and she thought with bitterness that it could not matter. How could they hear her so far away, and over the crowd, and when they were themselves quarreling in the tavern, and herself being carried farther away every minute?

"Ye'll not be taking a witch's word!" she cried out. "I am of the Kirk, and have been servant to Argyll himself!"

One or two of the nearest people hesitated doubtfully, for Argyll was a name to conjure with. But Mina dashed Kelpie's faint chance. "Aye!" she shrieked. "To be getting a bit of his hair for a hex! Look at her eyes, just!"

She was doomed, then. "Sons of the dogs!" she yelled once more, with despair in voice and heart. And then she was being shoved along with Mina and Bogle.

"*Chlanna non can, thigibh a so's gheibh sibh feoil!*" It was Ian's voice. A wedge began to cut itself into the crowd from behind, a bright blade gleaming, and Ian's wild face at the back of the sword.

And then another voice, that of Alex. "*Ian!*" it roared, and another wedge appeared behind the first. And now figures in MacDonald and Duncan bonnets cut a swathe, more swords gleamed, voices roared happily with the joy of battle.

But Alex was coming after Ian, and a black rage on his face, and his voice bellowing Ian's name. He was angry still, then, and the more so because Ian was trying to save her! Kelpie's feet were set against the cobblestones of the street, her body twisted to see behind. And now the hold on her was loosening as the witch-burners began to take alarm. But oh, would Ian be in time? Would Alex stop him?

Ian had nearly reached her. The crowd, mostly un-armed, swirled and shoved in disorganized fury. They turned from their victims now, and two or three dirks were flashed. The MacDonalds were gleefully wreaking havoc somewhere behind, but Alex had caught up with Ian now, and his face was fearful to look on. Ian's back was to Alex, his attention on dealing with those dirks still separating him from Kelpie. Kelpie could not see his hands, for the shoulders and heads in the way, but his face was grim, intent. "Hold on, Kelpie!" he shouted.

"*Ian!*" roared Alex again, and his sword rose—rose and then fell with a furious slash. And Ian was down, and his dark head had vanished in the crowd.

It was just as she had seen it in the loch! For an instant Kelpie felt nothing at all but a terrible cold emptiness, and then grief was in her very bones, and a small cry of anguish on her lips. She made a move toward the swarming, fighting spot where Ian had vanished. There was one brief glimpse of Alex, raging like one gone mad, and then the MacDonalds were there, making a havoc that sent townspeople screaming for safety. And somewhere, being trampled beneath, was the body of Ian, and perhaps she could reach him and help. . . .

And then she hesitated. Alex would be wanting to kill her too! And now was her chance to be away and safe from him. And after all, what good could she be to Ian? For either he was dead and past help, or, if not, there were the MacDonalds to care for him, and Maeve back at Perth.

Kelpie hesitated a moment longer, then she reverted to old habits and saved herself. She slipped like a hunted wildcat through the crowd, which now had other things on its mind than stopping her. She was out of it, around a corner, through the narrow streets in a swift streak of gray. The clamor grew muffled and scattered. She tore across the stone bridge and the moor and along a glen and over a hill. She ran until she could no longer breathe, and then crawled into a thick patch of broom and lay gasping and sobbing.

She must not think! She could not bear to think. Alex had really done it, then! The thing inside her had never really believed he would, and that was the thing now keening in black anguish that he could have done it.

And Ian! Was he dead, then? Dead trying to save herself, who had then fled without a backward look?

But it was only sense to have saved herself! It was what Ian had been trying to do, to save *her,* and wouldn't he have wished it? Why should it be the weight of a stone on her? Ian would have wished it, she told herself. And then she rolled over on her face and was violently sick.

How long had she been walking? And to where? It was just away from the town she had been going, and she was now far away, for she had spent more than one night in the heather. And yet she could not get away from the beating blackness in her mind.

Kelpie sank down in the drenched heather and discovered with vague surprise that rain was pouring steadily from a dreary sky. She looked wearily around and saw nothing but hills and heath closed in mist. She was wet as a water horse, and when had she last eaten?

What was she to do now? And where was she going? She didn't care much. It would be nice just to lie down and not be waking at all at all. But some inner vitality would never let her do that. She sighed. She must be finding food, then, and learning where she was. For all she knew, she might be back in Campbell country—and that thought roused her just a little.

She dragged herself to her feet and tramped on again. The glen ended in a long loch, so large that both ends were out of sight around the curves of the hills. Kelpie sat down again and thought, slowly, because she could not seem to think very well. There were not so many lochs of this size. She did not think she could have got so far as Loch Rannoch, and this seemed too long for Loch Earn and not wide enough for Loch Lomond. It must be that it was Loch Tay, and if this were so, then she might well be in Campbell country.

If only the sun would come out! If only there were some place that she could go and rest and hide away from the world and her thoughts . . .

And then she remembered the braes of Balquidder and two kind and lonely old folk who had said, "Haste ye back."

At this point Kelpie's instinct and gypsy training took over. Without stopping to wonder was she right or no, she turned to the left and trudged along the southern bank of the loch. She found berries and roots to eat. She lay down in the wet heather and slept, her plaidie around her, when she could go no farther. And then she awoke and went on. To the end oᶠ the loch she went, and down a glen, and around a mountain.

And late on a drizzly afternoon old Alsoon MacNab heard a faint scratch at her door and opened it to find her own plaidie back—wrapped round a morsel of wretched humanity that for once was not shamming in the least.

16. Morag Mhor

I<small>T WAS</small> pleasant to be cared for, pleasant and strange. Kelpie lay for several days on the pile of springy heather which served for her bed. At first she just slept and awoke to eat and sleep again. But then she began lying awake, her eyes on the smoky fire, or on the mortarless stone walls that leaned a little inward against the black rafters and thatched roof. Alsoon was always busy, cooking or sweeping the earthen floor with a besom broom or weaving or knitting, one eye always on her patient.

And why should they take her in and care for her so, when they had nothing to gain by it? Glenfern had done the same thing—no, best not to think of Glenfern, for that was too painful. She must learn to wall off those memories from her feelings, so that they would become like a witch-spot on the body, a spot that could feel no pain even though a pin was stuck in to the head. Kelpie had no witch-spots, though Mina did. But then, Kelpie was not a

witch, and what was more, she never would be, however
hard she might try!

The knowledge crept upon her stealthily, while she was
still too weak and drained to resist it. She had no power at
all. None of her spells had ever worked. And Mina had lied
about teaching her the Evil Eye. It came to her with bitter
clarity that the Evil Eye was a thing one must be born
with; it could never be learned. All Kelpie had was the
Second Sight, and many Highlanders had that.

She received the knowledge with a strange kind of in-
difference. Later, when she wasn't so tired, she would no
doubt feel a savage sense of loss. But she could not think
about it now—not yet.

Alsoon was bringing her some broth now and crooning
to her wee dark love to drink it and sleep. Callum must
have tramped far over the hills to find a deer to make it,
and they knew very well that she could never pay for it
at all, and they would be hurt even if she offered payment.
Highland hospitality was a warm, strong thing with rules
to it. It made a grace between host and guest and a bond
not to harm each other. This was why Alex had been so
angry at the way she left Glenfern, and Eithne so hurt,
and—and Ian—

She wrenched her mind from the thought of Ian, drank
her broth, and drifted back to sleep.

When she was on her feet again, Kelpie was strangely
content just to stay where she was. It seemed to her that

her life had been violently wrenched apart, and she hardly knew how to begin putting it back together again. She needed time to think. Kelpie had always found the world full and interesting, however cruel. She played a game. She avoided the cruelty when she could, and bore it if she must, and fought back when she had the chance. She adapted herself to each new situation that came along, and had quite enjoyed—on the whole—the glimpses of various new worlds that the last few months had offered.

But now she seemed to be cast out of every world she knew, for she could never go back to Glenfern, or to Mina and Bogle (even if she would), or to Campbell country. Worse, she did not even know what she wanted, now that the power of witchcraft was denied her. The old gypsy life no longer seemed attractive. New ideas had been planted in her mind, and she had found herself groping restlessly for something she could not name.

To keep her mind and hands busy, she began to help Alsoon and Callum with the various chores, and took an unexpected pleasure in them. For once, walls seemed not a trap but a warm, safe shelter from the early frost and biting wind outside, and from the world in general.

And so the autumn passed, and it was the dark of the year, with only a few brief hours of daylight and long gray dusks. In that remote glen they heard little of the outside world. It wasn't until she had been there for two months that a neighbor from over the hill came that way in search of stray cattle and stopped in to pass on the news that his brother had heard from someone's cousin who had been away in to a town.

Montrose had taken his army north to Aberdeen, and this time he had let his men sack the city. "It was because they had shot a wee drummer boy," explained the neighbor. "The lad was just along with the envoy, asking them would they like to send their women and bairns to safety. And Graham was so angry at it that he took the town and turned his army loose on it, but they say he was sorry after."

And then, it seemed, the old game of tag had started again, with Argyll panting after Montrose all the way from Bog o' Gight to Badenoch, Tumnel to Strathbogie, devastating lands as he went, and slaughtering people if he even suspected them of royalist sympathies.

When Kelpie awoke the next morning, she saw the white light of the first snow coming through the cracks in the shutters, and her first, unbidden thought was: did Ian lie somewhere beneath that blanket? Had Alex been punished for killing him? Where was Montrose now, and what was happening in Scotland? It was the beginning of a new restlessness and a growing desire to learn whether Ian *was* dead, and perhaps even to take vengeance herself on Alex, if no one else had done it already. Even without magic powers, she reflected with narrowed eyes, she could still use her wee *sgian dhu!*

The dark, smoky shieling became too cramped for such thoughts, and, in spite of the cold, Kelpie took to making long walks over the braes and around the foot of Ben More. Alsoon looked at her wisely. If she guessed that confusing thoughts were disturbing the young waif, she said nothing but merely finished whatever task Kelpie might have left undone when the restlessness was upon her.

"Och, and you'll be away again one day," predicted old Callum mildly one crisp afternoon when Kelpie paused at the sheep pen where he was working. " 'Tis the wanderlust you have in your feet—but are you not also wanting somewhere to call home?"

Kelpie had never thought of the matter. She did so now. What *was* a home? For Ian it had been Glenfern, where his heart stayed wherever the rest of him might be. But for Kelpie, Glenfern was not just a place; it was a feeling and it was people. It was Wee Mairi's bonnie face and confiding smile; and the twins crowding close, bright-eyed, to demand more stories; and Eithne's quick sympathy; and laughter beside the loch. It was teasing and love and trust among them all, and her own heart given recklessly against her better judgement.

No, home was not a place but a feeling—a deceitful feeling, she remembered bitterly. She had endangered Wee Mairi by her very affection, and Ian had trusted too much. . . . And Kelpie thought again that if Glenfern had not settled the score with Alex, she herself might do it one day. She thought of Mina and Bogle too, and hoped fiercely that they had not escaped.

There was more heavy snow the next week, and now this was nearly the longest time she had ever spent in one place—except for Glenfern, and Glenfern had been much more lively. She longed more and more for excitement, for adventure, aye, even for danger, for these were the spice of life. And so she stiffened with anticipation on the morning that wee Angus MacNab came racing over the hill toward the shieling hut. Important news was in his every movement.

"Och, Callum, and have you seen it?" he demanded in a shrill shout. "Montrose himself it is, and his army, just yon over the braes on the edge of Campbell land. It is said they will be going to harry Mac Cailein Mor in his own castle!"

Kelpie had been standing over near the sheep pen, very still, watching the small lad come. A too large kilt flapped about his knobbly knees, and himself and his long shadow and his twisting track were all dark against the white of the snow. To her left was the black of the shieling hut, smoke rising vaguely against the pearl-blue of the sky, and Callum standing by the door. Everything seemed to stop in time for just an instant, while something inside Kelpie awoke, stretched, looked around, and made a decision.

She didn't ask herself any questions then, but turned

in her tracks and walked back to the hut, where Callum and Alsoon were greeting the lad and asking for more details.

"And where are they?" she demanded.

Angus waved a skinny arm toward the north. "Yon, near Loch Tay. The clan is called out and will be joining there. I wish I could be going!"

Sudden reasonless elation filled Kelpie. She wrapped her plaidie more firmly about her shoulders and looked at Callum and Alsoon. "I'm away," she announced.

"Och, no, heart's darling!" protested Alsoon. "Not into Campbell lands, and in midwinter! Bide with us a wee while longer, until spring."

"I'm away," repeated Kelpie, a little sharply, as she realized that once again she was in danger of giving her heart. "And what harm from cold or Campbells when the army and all the women and bairns are along? I cannot bide longer, for my feet have the urge in them." And she tossed her dark head like a young Highland pony, so that the thick braids—well tended by Alsoon—leaped over her shoulders and beat against her waist, as if impatient.

Alsoon sighed. "Well, then, and you must go if you must. But come away in first, my light, and I'll be giving you food to take along. Dried venison there is, and fresh bannocks, and oatcakes. And here are the new skin brogans that Callum has finished for you."

"Haste ye back, white love," she added at last as Kelpie

took the food and put on the shoes and stood looking at
her.

"Aye," said Kelpie, and her heart was torn. The Mac-
Nabs gave and asked no return but to be able to give
more. "You've been kind, and I not deserving it," she
murmured, and then clenched her fists and walked quickly
out of the low doorway, lest she be caught up in folly
again.

Halfway up the hill she paused, stared back at the long,
low shieling hut, and then waved at the two old people
standing there. Tears stung her eyelids for a moment, and
impulsively she crooked her forefinger, calling down a
blessing upon them.

Five minutes later she had shaken off her sadness. She
lifted her head and breathed the air of new adventure.
The hills had been calling this long while, calling through
the spell of black depression that was on her. But the spell
was broken now, and she was answering the call.

At the top of the hill she was seized by fresh exuberance.
Curving her arms upward like a stag's antlers, she broke
into the light, wild leaps of a dance that the Highland
men did around the campfire or at friendly gatherings,
and then laughed aloud at her own impertinence—she, a
lass, to be doing a man's dance, and doing it well too.
The dance took on a distinctly mocking and impudent
quality.

From the top of the next hill she looked down on Montrose's army, which had made camp by the loch. From the mouth of the glen, the MacNabs were arriving, great-kilts swinging about their bare, strong knees, and the top halves of the kilts wrapped round massive shoulders. Kelpie surveyed the scene for a moment before going down, counting tartans. MacDonalds were still most plentiful, with Gordons, MacPhersons, Stewarts—but she saw no Cameron tartans.

She also saw no children, and only a small scattering of women. Where were they all, then? Frowning a little, she went down, over the snowy hillside, to the camp.

"Whist, lass, and what is it you're wanting?" It was a bearded Irish MacDonald. "The time for sweethearts' farewells is past, and we off to raid and harry the Camp-bells in their lair." The beard split in a grin of vengeful glee.

"It is I that am coming with you," announced Kelpie cheekily. "Where are all the women and bairns?"

He stared. "Back at Blair Castle, the most of them, safe in Stewart country. It is only a few of the strongest, and they with no children, that we have brought. 'Tis no adventure for you, lassie. Be away back home."

"I am strong, and with no bairns," argued Kelpie. "And I'm frightened to travel alone." She looked helpless and pleading. "I have no home, and I'd like well to raid the Campbells. Can I not be coming?"

He grinned sympathetically. "Och, well—we've a

bloody enough work to do, and might even use an extra
nurse once or twice. Go find Morag Mhor, then, who is
head of the women."

Kelpie recognized Morag Mhor as soon as she saw her—
the tall, gaunt woman she had noticed at Blair Atholl,
who well deserved the title of "great" Morag. Ragged
woolen skirts were kilted up over a bright red petticoat,
showing ankles as sturdy as a man's. The worn Gordon
plaidie had fallen back from her head, and her face was
more alive than it had been at Blair Atholl, but as fierce
as ever. When Kelpie found her, she was berating a red-
faced MacGregor at least two inches shorter than she,
who clearly had no fight left in him.

"And don't be crossing my path again until I feel for-
giving, or I'll box the other ear!" she finished briskly and
then turned to look at Kelpie. "Gypsy!" she said, crossing
brawny arms on her breast.

"Indeed and no!" protested Kelpie with great prompt-
ness. "Only a poor lost lass, and away from home—"

Morag Mhor laughed loudly. "Gypsy!" she repeated,
pointing a long forefinger.

Kelpie regarded her warily and trimmed her tale. "The
gypsies were stealing me when I was a bairn," she conceded, not expecting to be believed.

"Aye, then," agreed Morag Mhor surprisingly. "Because
of the ringed eyes of you, I think. You'll have the Second
Sight. Are you a witch?"

"Are you?" countered Kelpie, remembering with a pang that she herself was not and never could be.

Morag shrugged wide shoulders. "I have a healing power. But I'm not belonging to any coven of daft folk who hold Black Mass and dance their silly feet off at midnights. My power is in what I'm doing, not what I'm saying." Her lined face drew down fiercely. "I'll be helping to put the curse of deeds on the Campbells this week. They passed my happy wee home in Gordon country and left behind a blackened stone—and I arriving back from over the hill to find the thatch still smoldering, and my man dead, and my son beside him, and the lad not yet ten! I have thirsted for Campbell blood ever since, and I shall drink deep."

She stopped, staring into the white distance with eyes that were of burning stone. Kelpie reflected that she would not like to have this woman for an enemy. Best to go canny.

"I was prisoner of Mac Cailein Mor," she volunteered. "He would have burned me, but I escaped."

"Och, then, and you're another who hates him!" Morag's eyes returned from unpleasant places. "Stay along with me, then, gypsy lass. We'll see revenge together, and no man nor devil will harm you whilst I am near." And Kelpie believed her.

17. The Road to Inverary

THEY had slept on the border of Campbell country, after feeding on Campbell cattle collected by some twenty or thirty Highlanders. Their tightly woven woolen plaids had helped to keep out the cold, and so had the fires scattered along the glen. But Kelpie was glad enough of the red wool hose that Alsoon had knitted for her, and of the warm bulk of Morag beside her.

Now they were heading up Strath Fuile, and the warm-hearted comradeship of the Highlanders became a savage expectation, for here at last was the great enemy ahead. Montrose might talk all he liked of getting to the border to aid the King in England—but a score or two must be settled first. Montrose had had to compromise; otherwise too many of his army would have just slipped away home, taking with them as many stolen cattle as possible.

Now an advance party had gone ahead of the main

army to find cattle before the owners could be warned and drive them off to hide in the hills. And Morag Mhor, with a dark and unpleasant grin, had attached herself and Kelpie to them. The men, knowing of her murdered husband and child, let her join them, with a grim jest or two about the fate of any Campbells unlucky enough to run into her.

They rounded a curve in the river, and there before them was a long, low shieling hut with two children playing out in front and a handful of cattle scattered up the hill behind. Morag saw the hut first and was off toward it with a flash of red petticoat. Kelpie wished suddenly that she had stayed with the rest of the women, but she hurtled after Morag simply because it didn't occur to her to do anything else. Now the men had seen it too, and a menacing yell rose from thirty throats as some of them raced around after the cattle, and the rest—mostly Irish MacDonalds—followed Morag and Kelpie toward the hut.

Even as she was running, the thing inside Kelpie felt sick at what was to come. Campbells they were, certainly, but what fault had the bairns committed? Montrose would be angry, surely, with his scruples about making war on the innocent. Now the children had seen them and were running toward the house, screaming with terror. An ashen-faced woman gathered them to her and then paused in the doorway, uncertain whether to run inside or away into the hills. Kelpie could almost taste the fear in her.

Then Kelpie's foot hit something soft and yielding. She tripped and flew head first into a patch of wet snow. There was a wail of pain and—the cry of a small child.

Kelpie raised her head from the snow in time to see Morag stop, whirl, and race back toward Kelpie and the child. Was she going to begin her revenge by killing the bairn?

"Is it hurt that you are?" roared Morag, but she was not speaking to Kelpie. She picked up the crying child and stood, her gaunt face twisted with the conflict of feelings going on in her. Then she turned to Kelpie, with the Irish MacDonalds only a few yards from them. "Come on!" she ordered and raced with the child toward the hut and the cowering woman.

Bewildered, Kelpie scrambled up and followed, just barely ahead of the men. Morag thrust the baby into its mother's arms, whirled, and drew her *sgian dhu*.

"You'll not be touching them, whatever!" she bellowed at the astonished giant who led the pack. "Back, or I'll skewer you, Rab MacDonald! Am I not a woman and mother myself? A plague on men and war! Back, I say!"

She was terrifying; her avenging fury turned to defense of her prey. It was altogether too much for the Highlanders. They stood and stared, a full dozen of them in a semicircle before her.

"Fine brave soldiers ye are!" jeered Morag. "Are ye no afraid to be attacking such dangerous foes? Here's the wee bairn, now. Will one of you not challenge him to fair combat?"

They shuffled their feet, quite taken aback. The madness that Morag herself had kindled in them trickled out, to be replaced by the Highland sense of the ridiculous. One of them chuckled, and then several others began to roar with laughter. "And is this your own vengeance, Morag Mhor?" they hooted. "I will be remembering this the next time you are clouting me on the ear and send for a bairn to protect me," added the giant called Rab.

Morag Mhor seemed not to care about the teasing. She stood guard over the grateful little family while the cattle were caught and while the rest of the army arrived on the scene. And, with the backing of Montrose, she defied those who wanted to burn the house.

"I can do no more for ye," she told the Campbell woman when the army and its captured cattle had started on once again. "You have your bairns and your home—although your Campbell army left me neither, nor husband. I intended to do the same to you, but I could not, for I saw myself in you, and it came to me that a woman's place is to give life, not to take it. It comes to me, too, that men are a senseless lot with all their useless killing, and perhaps we mothers should be raising our sons to different ideas."

And then she turned abruptly and headed in long strides back to the Highland army, not waiting for the stammered words of thanks.

Kelpie trailed along at her heels, saying nothing but thinking a good deal.

And so it went, along to Tyndrum and up Glenorchy. Morag Mhor vehemently defended every woman and child they found, against the threats and wild arguments of the Highland soldiers. It didn't take Kelpie long to discover that all this was a great act put on by the Highlanders for Morag's benefit, and it was a surprise to her that a woman as shrewd as Morag didn't know it too. But she never guessed.

"I know you for the braw liar you are," remarked Kelpie saucily to Rab one morning over their beef-and-oatmeal breakfast. "You will be teasing her every time, and you as softhearted as herself."

"As ever was," agreed Rab, rolling a dark eye at her. "But do not be telling Morag, whatever, for it is not just teasing. With the grief of her, she is needing something to fight, but she is happier to be fighting us to save bairns than the other way around."

Although the campaign through Campbell territory was less bloodthirsty than Kelpie had expected, still it was not pretty. Men of fighting age found little mercy, few cattle escaped the voracious appetite of the army, and more than a few barns and thatch roofs went up in smoke behind it.

Blazing fires and roasted meat were good at night, after long and cold marches. Since there were so few women to do the cooking, the men helped too, with good will and bantering. Kelpie poked at a haunch of beef one chill but clear evening, thinking to herself that they were going a long way round to Argyll at Inverary, in a huge triangle to north and west. Surely by now Argyll would have received word of this invasion! Kelpie wondered what he would be doing about it. The obvious thing would be to come away after them, and she looked apprehensively toward the purple-black hills that surrounded the orange firelight.

"Is there food for a starving— Why, 'tis the water witch!" Kelpie turned to face Archie MacDonald, whose black eyes were sparkling with curiosity. They stared at each other.

"And where did you vanish to that day?" he demanded. "A braw lot of trouble and grief you caused! If you've the power to vanish into thin air, you might have been doing it before Ian Cameron was cut down trying to save you."

Kelpie winced. "Was he killed entirely?" she asked, her heart pounding for fear of the answer.

"Na, na, not entirely. But a nasty wound it was. Still, he survived it, although he had to go back to Glenfern, and no more fighting for the time." Kelpie saw again in her mind the savage downward sweep of Alex's broadsword and had to push aside the tumult of feelings that it brought. But—Ian was not dead! Alex had not killed him!

"And Alex MacDonald?" she demanded balefully.

"He's—away," said Archie, and it was clear that he was

going to say no more. But then, he was Alex's cousin and
not likely to want to speak of it. At least Kelpie knew now
that Alex had not been hanged, and she thought again that
she might be the one to avenge Ian some day. For she
doubted that, even now, Ian himself would raise a hand
against Alex. She looked right through Archie, and her
slanted blue eyes held no very pleasant expression.

The meat was done now and being divided. Archie
pulled his *sgian dhu* from his stocking, vanished briefly
into the crowd of hungry men, and emerged with a smok-
ing hunk for Kelpie in one hand and one for himself in
the other. She bit into the meat hungrily and then looked
up to find the deep black eyes still fixed on her, and a
question in them.

"That day," he began, with an uncertain note in his
voice, "were you sending a call in the mind to Alex before
you gave the Cameron rant with your voice?"

Kelpie looked as blank as she felt. "I don't understand
you whatever!" she said warily.

"Why," he began, and frowned a little, "there we were
in the tavern, with Alex and Ian in a fury at each other,
and none of us even hearing the sounds outside. It was a
braw quarrel, with Ian gone white with the anger in him,
and Alex the color of a rowan berry. And then Alex was
stopping in mid-word, with an intent, listening look on the
face of him, and looking round. And it was because of his

silence that an instant later we were hearing the Cameron rant, and Ian shouting ' 'Tis Kelpie in trouble!' "

Kelpie shook her head blankly. "And what then?" was all she said.

Archie shrugged. "Why, then, Ian forgot the quarrel and was away out the door, and Alex after him with drawn sword, and the rest of us collected our wits and followed, not knowing if Alex's black fury was still for Ian, or for the witch-hunters. His face was a fearful thing to see, and I'm hoping I never meet the like in battle, for 'twould be the end of me. But you know the rest better than I. How was it, Kelpie, that Alex heard you even through the quarrel, and before the rest of us?"

"I don't know," said Kelpie absently, her mind on another question altogether. For the thing she had suspected was clear. It was herself had helped bring about the scene in the loch, and hatred of her had caused Alex to strike down his foster brother. It was the only possible explanation, and there was a sore hurt in the thought of it. How could Alex have hated her that much, who had never seemed to hate her at all, but only scorn her? Her short upper lip curled. Och, he would pay for it, just! Even though Kelpie could no longer hope for witchcraft to help her, he would pay for it.

Archie looked at her uneasily. There was a look about her not quite canny, and it was occurring to him that folk

called after water witches, who could communicate without the voice, might not be a braw choice for companionship, so he brought her another hunk of meat—to avoid
offending her—and melted hastily into the crowd of soldiers.

The army passed the very spot near Loch Awe where
Kelpie had first seen Janet Campbell that June day six
months ago. And then they were heading at last toward
Inverary, through the steep wilds of Glen Aray where she
and Janet had gone. And what had been happening to
Janet all this time? she wondered. Not that she really
cared, she tried to tell herself, except that Janet was a
harmless soul and not deserving to be harmed by either
Mac Cailein Mor or his enemies.

There was no detour to the top of the hill this time.
Straight down the glen the army came, pipes shrieking
in ominous triumph. It was a braw sound indeed, a wild
song that set the blood running with joyful madness—or
the blood of Montrose's army, at any rate. Kelpie wondered briefly how it sounded to the ears in Inverary. Along
the river they marched, half running now, and erupted
into the valley, the town of Inverary seeming to cower
ahead on its point of land, and the castle—so familiar to
Kelpie—to the left.

Morag Mhor was with the men heading for the village,
loudly daring them to lay a finger on woman or child, her

voice rising as they insisted, grinning, that this time every wee babe would be slaughtered, just. For once, this game had no interest for Kelpie, and she headed straight for the castle. If Mac Cailein Mor was captured, she wanted to be there to gloat.

Everywhere there was clear evidence of surprise and panic. The town and castle, unaware of the approaching invasion, had been celebrating the Christmas season—in their sober Puritan way, of course, with longer and more frequent sermons. Kelpie's lip curled with scorn for a chief so feckless as not to know what was happening in his own country—or else so sure of his invulnerability that he took no precautions. Och, she could hardly wait to see him taken prisoner! Her small white teeth fairly glittered in her smile.

She had just reached the castle wall when a shout of dismay and fury broke out. Kelpie rushed to a high knoll where she could see. Men were pointing to the small bay. A fishing boat was hastily heading out into the loch.

" 'Tis himself is running away!" And Kelpie hardly needed a second glance to confirm it. Her keen eyes picked out two red heads, the short bulk of Lady Argyll, the patch of Cameron tartan that was Ewen.

"Ssss!" said Kelpie in savage regret.

The pipes lifted a wild wail of derision. "Oh, the great Argyll!" someone yelled. "Brave General Campbell! What,

will you be away off, Mac Cailein Mor, and us just come
to visit?"

Montrose wasted no time fuming over what couldn't be
helped, although he must have been bitterly disappointed.
The capture of Argyll this day might have changed history
—although he had not the Second Sight to tell him how
much. Even Kelpie did not know, for the crystal had not
yet showed her the scene to come later, when Montrose
himself calmly mounted the scaffold.

His face was calm now as he gave orders to set about
taking the castle abandoned by its owner. It wasn't as
difficult as it might have been. One couldn't expect in-
spired defense from the men who had been left behind
while their leader fled. And once Montrose's men were in
full possession, Kelpie entered the castle through those
massive gates she had passed through before—but this
time with an arrogant sway to her slim body.

She wasted no time with the fine white bread and wine
that had been discovered, nor even with the miserable
figure of Mrs. MacKellar huddled on a chair in the hall.
She knew where she was going, and she wanted to be
the first one there.

Argyll's apartments were deserted. She walked boldly
through the massive oaken doors, on into the inner chamber. There was a fine large cairngorm brooch on the table,
mounted in silver, bigger than her fist. Fine, that! She
looked around. What else?

A thought struck her. The next chamber must be that of Lady Argyll. In she went, and in a moment was kneeling beside a chest of fine gowns. A pity there were none of bright colors. Kelpie had always wanted a gown of flame-red velvet, but of course such a thing would never be found in a Covenant household. Still, there was one of moss-green, and the softest, finest wool she had ever seen, and not so *very* much too big, provided she belted it tightly about the waist. And she laughed with joy. Here was the fine silver belt she had always wanted.

Next she pulled out a lovely cloak the color of juniper— and she must have it, although it was lined with Campbell tartan—and a silken purse, a linen kerchief, and several baubles. She tried on a pair of square-toed leather shoes with silver buckles, but they hurt her feet sorely, so she kicked them off and went back into Argyll's room for a silver snuff box she had seen there.

And as she stood, green gown bunched about her waist under untidy thick braids (uncombed since leaving Alsoon), the cairngorm in one hand and the snuff box in the other, the outer door opened.

For an instant memory played tricks on her and she thought that it was Mac Cailein Mor finding her there with the hairs in her hand, and blind panic was on her. Then it cleared as a voice spoke.

"*Dhé!*" boomed Antrim. "And whom have we here?"

" 'Tis the eavesdropping lass from last summer,"

answered Montrose, standing still, taking in every detail.

Kelpie looked back at him fearlessly. He was amused, she could tell. And besides, did not his scruples prevent him from harming women or children, even enemy ones, and she no enemy?

"I see you've wasted no time," he observed mildly. "How is it you're here ahead even of your army commander?"

"I was knowing the way and wanting to be first," explained Kelpie artlessly. She waved her loot at him with great pride in her cleverness.

He looked at it, and at her. The corners of his mouth moved slightly. "That would be Argyll's cairngorm, I suppose?"

She nodded, regarding it happily. Then something occurred to her, and she glanced up at him dubiously from under her thick lashes. Perhaps it might be wise to sacrifice material gain—if necessary—for policy.

"Were you wanting it yourself?" she asked reluctantly. "I will give it to you, if you like. There's another nearly as good in yon box," she added, "and this a wee bit heavy for a lass to be wearing."

Montrose laughed. "No, I don't want Argyll's brooch," he assured her, to her relief. Then he looked at her seriously. "I don't suppose it's ever occurred to you," he suggested, "that stealing could be a bad thing?"

"Och, aye!" exclaimed Kelpie earnestly, "You must be

very canny at it, my Lord, and lucky, too. For 'tis a bad thing indeed and indeed to be caught! But Mac Cailein Mor's away in his wee boat, and no danger now."

This time it was Antrim who boomed with laughter, and Kelpie looked at him resentfully. Clearly he had had no experience at getting caught, or he would never be laughing at such a serious matter.

"I didn't mean quite that, although I'm sure it must be true," explained Montrose gently, and the corners of his mouth were jiggling again. "I mean, did you never think that it might be wrong to steal, whether you were caught at it or no?"

"Och, no!" said Kelpie, wide-eyed. "But then, perhaps 'tis different for you," she added kindly. "Being a chief and lord and all, you will be able to get things without stealing them, and I doubt you're ever hungry, whatever."

Montrose sighed. "Aye," he agreed, seeming sad for some reason. " 'Tis different for me. You'd best run along now, though." And he turned to look after her as she left the room.

Kelpie went back to the other wing, picked up an item or two from Mrs. MacKellar's room, and then stood still for a minute, frowning at nothing at all. Why did people persist in making her think about new and uncomfortable ideas? A few months ago she would have been genuinely puzzled by the notion that it might be wrong to steal, even though a body was not caught at it. But now, even though she had pretended not to know what Montrose meant, the idea wasn't really as startling as it would once have been. It was the sort of thing the folks at Glenfern might have said, or Ewen Cameron, or even Alsoon and Callum. It undoubtedly had to do with the integrity thing Alex and Ian talked of, and all of them wanting her to apply it to herself. Why should she? Mina and Bogle had taught her that anything was right if one got away with it—but then, Mina and Bogle were evil, and perhaps everything they said was wrong.

Kelpie sighed. On the other hand, Alex talked about those ideas, and he was evil too. So what was a lass to think, at all?

She wandered down into the main hall, which was still a chaos of triumphant men. But she was so engrossed in her problem of right and wrong that she quite forgot to taunt the dejected and weeping Mrs. MacKellar. In any case, it no longer seemed necessary. After all, the house-keeper had been loyal to her chief, and it the only safe thing to do—but would it not be safer now for her to side with the royalist victors?

Kelpie frowned at the red-eyed and unlovely figure of Mrs. MacKellar, for in it there was something undefeated and almost gallant. No, Mrs. MacKellar would never change sides, but would stay loyal to Mac Cailein Mor, even though he was not worthy of it. Why? Did she fear that he would come back? Or was this something like not stealing, that a body did even against his own interest? Was that what integrity was? But what good was it? As far as Kelpie could see, it was more likely to be a nuisance than an asset.

She wandered over to one of the deep-set windows and stared out, unseeing, her whole attention focused on her thoughts. The folk at Glenfern, like Mrs. MacKellar, would remain loyal for always to a person or ideal. This was part of the thing about them which she had sensed from the first—the daftness, the difference. True they would be, whether or not it was profitable or safe, aye, though it cost them their lives—all but Alex. And it was this, perhaps, that had shocked her so. For Alex, surely, would never change sides but would be true to an ideal—and how was it, then, that he could betray a friend?

She leaned her forehead against one of the thick diamond-shaped panes, dimming it even more with her breath, and remembered that Montrose had talked of such things back at Blair Atholl. But neither he nor anyone else had ever explained to Kelpie why this way of acting was desirable. Was it possible that there was some strange kind of happiness in it? Did they have things inside which would make them uncomfortable if they acted otherwise?

Kelpie stopped trying to understand, for she found that there was an argument going on within her. The thing inside her was saying that this was a fine and proud way to be, but her common sense told her that it was not at all practical, and had she not vowed to think of herself first, last, and always? And surely if it was a choice between her own safety and any other thing (and she forced the thought of Wee Mairi from her mind), surely it would be only sensible to look out for herself, as ever was!

18. The Black Sail

KELPIE awoke from a dream in which she was trudging along beside a loch against blinding rain. She blinked a little as she remembered that she was back at Inverlochy Castle—the same place she and Mina and Bogle had spent the first night after leaving Glenfern. She shivered a little, partly at the memory of Mina and Bogle, and partly from cold. Hugging the stolen cloak and her old plaidie about her, she hurried down the tower stairs and out to the central court, where Morag Mhor and the other women were preparing breakfast.

"Slugabed!" Morag greeted her, and Kelpie grinned cheekily, knowing all about Morag's pretended fierceness by now. There were more men than ever to feed, since the Glencoe MacDonalds and the Stewarts of Appin had joined, and Kelpie was glad that they were in friendly Cameron country, where it was safe to build fires and they

could have hot porridge. She had got heartily tired of a
diet of oatmeal mixed with cold water. She looked thoughtfully up at Ben Nevis, which looked larger and more lowering under its quilt of snow than in the green and tawny
blanket of summer, and realized suddenly that she had
had enough of army life.

Rab paused by the fire to sniff the oatmeal hungrily and
announce that he thought he would just go out and lift
some cattle for breakfast. He chucked Morag Mhor under
the chin as he said it, and received a sound clout on the
ear as a reward. "Ouch!" he exclaimed, making a great
show of nursing his ear. "You will ever be bullying me,
Morag *avic,* and I a poor helpless man at your mercy."

Kelpie giggled, and Morag shook her fist at the other
ear. "This is the day we go to ask Lochiel and the Camerons to join us, and you would be lifting their cattle!
Amadan!"

Rab began explaining that they didn't really need the
Camerons at all, but Kelpie stopped listening, for she was
thinking that this would be a good time indeed to leave
the army. She had had enough of battles. Just a few miles
up the Great Glen was the pass that led to Glenfern.
Would she be welcome there? Surely Ian would remember
that she had warned him against Alex, and so would forgive her for running away and leaving him struck down
and half dead. Would he and his father join Montrose?
she wondered. Or would Lochiel dare to raise his clan?

She turned to Morag Mhor, who had sent Rab, protesting, out to the river for more water, and was now vigorously stirring the porridge. "Lochiel would be daft to call out his clan," she suggested. "With his grandson in Campbell hands, he could not dare."

Morag thought about it for a while, her lean face still and expressionless. "There was a wise woman in our village long ago," she said at last, "who used to say to me, 'Always dare to do what is right,' and I am thinking Lochiel will say the same. Would you understand that, Kelpie?"

"No!" said Kelpie forcefully and scowled. Ewen Cameron himself had used those same words. So here again were those ideas that she did not want to think about. She set her small face into a hard mask and dropped the subject. "I am thinking I have had my fill of armies and battles," she announced. "I will stay behind when you go up the Great Glen, and perhaps go to stay with friends here in Lochaber."

"Well, then, and a blessing on you," said Morag. "May you find a home for your bones and your spirit—though I think you will never stay in one place for long. I'm thinking I'll go back to Gordon country myself soon. No doubt there are orphans left by the Campbells who would be needing a mother."

Kelpie followed the army as far as Lochiel's home at Torcastle, curious to see whether or not Lochiel would

raise his clan. He did. The traditional cross was made of
two sturdy sticks bound firmly together. And according
to the ancient ceremony the ends were set aflame, extinguished in goat's blood, then lighted once more: one of
Lochiel's men held the cross proudly high and set off
at a trot that carried him deeper into Cameron territory.
The torch would be passed from runner to runner until
the whole area had received the message of war.

The army stayed at Torcastle for two days while Camerons came flocking to the call of their chief. If any had
misgivings about Argyll's possible revenge on them, they
did not show it; nor did Lochiel, that stern old man who
held his head so high. Kelpie did not wait to see the
Glenfern Camerons arrive, for she had sudden misgivings
about seeing Ian again. Instead, she went back to the
tower room at Inverlochy Castle in a very thoughtful
frame of mind.

For several days she stayed at the castle, enjoying her
solitude, and getting her food from homes nearby with
surprising ease. For the very people who had once regarded her with deep suspicion were now delighted to
give food and hospitality to the wistful lass who had been
a prisoner of Argyll, who had been helped by Ewen Cameron himself, and who had even got away with Lady
Argyll's fine cloak. Food, scanty though it might be with
the men away in the army, was shared, and there was not
a home where she was not urged to bide awhile.

But she shook her black head. Och, no, she said. She was away up the Glen. But she would take her leave marveling at such openheartedness to a stranger—even one who had not yet stolen anything. After thinking about it, Kelpie decided not to take anything at all. Somehow the good will seemed more valuable than anything she might steal.

Then the mild weather turned into sudden bitter cold. The night wind hurled blasts of snow against the tower walls, crept up the winding stairs, and whined outside like the banshee. It was so cold that Kelpie thought she might put away misgivings and go to Glenfern after all. Surely Lady Glenfern would not refuse her shelter in this cold!

She was heading back to Inverlochy in the early dusk when she decided this. Her stomach was comfortably full of hot broth and scones from a generous young Cameron wife, she was a trifle sleepy, and it would be good indeed to sleep tomorrow night or the next in the comfort of Glenfern, under the same roof with Wee Mairi.

It was fortunate that Kelpie's senses remained alert even when her mind was on other things. Even so, she had nearly walked up to the castle gate before she realized that something was wrong, and she never knew exactly what it was that warned her. But suddenly she stopped, alive to the sharp feel of danger, her small figure dark and taut against the faintly luminous patches of snow. An instant later she simply was not there, and the Campbell soldier who came running out of the gate, under the impression that he had seen something, shook his head and cursed the weather.

Kelpie lay in the snow where she had thrown herself behind a small hillock, not daring to raise her head but listening as if her life depended on it—which it did. Soon there was no doubt. Inverlochy Castle was being occupied—by Mac Cailein Mor and his army!

With sick dismay she pieced things together. Someone called for Campbell of Auchinbreck. Then there was a harsh and authoritative Lowland voice. And by crouching behind a thick clump of juniper and twisting her head cautiously, Kelpie could just make out a galley with black sails silhouetted against the gray waters of the Loch.

Oh, there was no doubt whatever! The Campbell had gathered his courage and his army and had come after Montrose.

19. Footprints in the Snow

KELPIE spent the night at the shieling hut of Lorne Cameron, which was nestled at the foot of Ben Nevis. Lorne had urged Kelpie to stay, for she and her four bairns were alone since her husband had gone off with Montrose and his army. Now her ruddy young face paled at Kelpie's news.

"Campbells! *Dhé!* and they will be murdering us all, then!"

"Perhaps not," said Kelpie hopefully. "If Mac Cailein Mor is after Montrose, perhaps he'll not be lingering in Lochaber."

But she slept with one ear well out of the folds of her plaidie, cocked for any sounds of danger. The hut was only a mile or so from Inverlochy Castle, and if Lorne had

reason to fear Mac Cailein Mor, Kelpie had that much
more.

She had planned to be off the first thing in the morning,
out of danger. But somehow she found herself waiting,
even after she had eaten the hot oatmeal Lorne cooked,
and tucked some food into her pouch. There was Lorne
here, and the wee ones, and none of Kelpie's concern at all.
But Lorne was frightened and uncertain what to do, and
they so helpless and looking up to Kelpie—and after all,
perhaps it would be wise just to take a wee peek at what
Argyll was doing, and see the size of his army.

"You might just be getting food and blankets together in
case you need to hide," she suggested. "And I'll go have a
look around."

"Och, 'tis both good and brave you are!" said Lorne
gratefully. Kelpie left the house hurriedly, feeling oddly
embarrassed.

She moved cautiously around the flank of the ben, skulking behind masses of juniper and pine clumps, until she
could see the castle. *Mise-an-dhui!* It was an army indeed
and indeed! Highland Campbells and Lowlanders too, and
well more than twice what Montrose could have, even
with his new recruits. But Argyll seemed to be making no
move to follow him up the Great Glen, even with this
advantage.

Kelpie's heart sank as she watched groups of men form-
ing before the castle. It was what she had expected in the

heart of her. Mac Cailein Mor had no heart for battle but would be about his usual practice of wiping out women and children. Even now one of the groups of soldiers was setting off toward the little cluster of homes on the edge of Loch Linnhe, and another was turning west along Loch Eil.

She watched no longer but headed back around the northern side of Ben Nevis. In a way this might be fortunate for her, giving her time to be up the Great Glen ahead of them. But suppose they penetrated as far as Glenfern? Perhaps she ought to be heading eastward, and out of the way altogether. In any case she would be passing Lorne's home on the way, and it costing only a few minutes to warn the lass. Nor was this just profitless foolishness, she told herself, for who knew when she might be needing a friend under obligation to herself?

An hour later she was laboring up the side of the mountain with a bundle of food in one arm and the next-smallest bairn in the other; Lorne, with the baby, and the older children panting behind. "Mind ye stay clear of soft snow," she warned over her shoulder. "It could be putting them on your trail."

Another hour saw them settled in a well-hidden shepherd's shelter, cold and uncomfortable and not daring to have a fire, but at least safer than at their home.

"Will you not be staying too?" begged Lorne, her dark eyes anxious for the safety of this generous new friend.

But Kelpie shook her head. She wanted to be farther than this from Argyll. And besides, a new thought was beginning to hound the fringes of her mind. Montrose, all unknowing, was now between two armies, for was not Seaforth at Inverness with five thousand men? And if he should be caught in a trap and wiped out, it would put Argyll altogether in control of the Highlands as well as Lowlands—and what would happen to Kelpie then? For her own safety, it seemed, she must try to warn Montrose.

It was a sore uncomfortable thought, filled with hardship and danger. She tried to put it out of her mind as she picked her way down the gaunt wintry slope, but it wouldn't leave. And with it were thoughts of Morag Mhor and Rab and Archie and Montrose himself lying slain in the snow, and all the comradeship and merry teasing silenced forever. A pity that would be. With a sigh she headed up the glen, a sharp eye out for any movement that might spell danger.

Och, then, but it was cold! Her feet were icy in their hide shoes, even with the woolen hose, and it was threatening to snow again. However could she catch up with the army at all? Perhaps it had already met Seaforth. But she kept on going.

She saw nothing but hares and deer and a lone eagle, until she reached the River Spean. Then a short, wiry figure came from the brush just ahead, and Kelpie sank swiftly to the ground for a tense moment before she saw he was not a Campbell. He was alone and in a faded Cameron kilt. Kelpie followed him to a dilapidated hut on the bank of the river and watched him enter. A drift of smoke began to rise. Might not he help himself and his clan by taking the message for her? And then she would be free to seek safety. She walked up to the door boldly.

"Come away in," came the expected lilt of Gaelic when she knocked, and the man's face turned to her in surprise as she entered. *"Dhia dhuit,"* he greeted her politely. "And what is a wee lass doing alone in the cold? Will you no have a sup of hot food?"

"I will, then," agreed Kelpie promptly. "And give an important word to you, and also a task if you will do it."

The man listened while she talked and ate, his face growing graver and grimmer. "Aye so," he agreed. " 'Tis the hand of destiny that I live alone here and knew nothing of the clan rising, or I would be with them, and a bad time of it you would be having alone and in this weather. Eat your fill, then, whilst I fill my pouch, and I'll be away before you're done. You can be biding here whilst I am gone."

"That I will not!" retorted Kelpie firmly. "For every house in Lochaber is a danger. I'll be away east out of trouble."

He frowned and shook his head. "There is no shelter to the east of here, lass, and it too cold to be sleeping out. And I have just come from hunting a wolf that has been

skulking upriver. You would be safer here, I am thinking,
for my house is alone and well hidden. But if you're feared
to rest here, there is a bittie cave nearby, and you are
welcome to my blankets and food. Follow the Spean along
up for a mile or so, and where the Cour is entering it turn
south for a bit and mark sharp the west bank. The cave is
in a high bluff and well hid with juniper. But I'm thinking
you'll be safe enough the night here, whatever, and it
nearly dark already. There'll be no Campbells along this
day, and 'tis no good for you to be freezing."

"Aye, then," agreed Kelpie, seeing the sense to this, and
the man was off. Odd, she didn't know the name of him,
nor he hers, and yet he was away on a dangerous errand
on her word. A purpose in common—or common danger
—she decided, was like a spell, binding even strangers one
to another.

The morning was heavy with clouds, the new snow a
dead white beneath the gray of the sky. Kelpie put out the
fire for fear of any betraying smoke and set out to locate
the cave, wishing she dared stay in the warmth of the
shieling. But as she trudged along the Cour River, watching the west bank, she stopped. Clear in the snow were
footprints coming down the Cour—and stopping just
ahead in a tumbled heap of snow. Kelpie stared, eyes
narrowed. Footsteps didn't just stop, unless someone had
wings.

No, there were no wings. There the prints went, back

the way they came. In a moment Kelpie had read the story. A man it was, by the size of the prints, and coming north along the Cour in a great hurry, so that he did not notice the treacherous slab of granite by the river, with ice under the snow. And there he had slipped and fallen; the mark was plain. Then, it would seem, he had made back the way he had come, limping sorely.

Kelpie straightened and looked up the glen cautiously. Where was he, then? And who was he? Warily she began to follow the retreating footprints.

They angled up the hill to the right presently, through a thick patch of pine and juniper. Kelpie hesitated, peering through it, her right hand reaching for the *sgian dhu* in the front of her dress, feet ready to run. Nothing stirred. And then a tiny trickle of smoke floated up just a few feet away from behind the brush. *Dhé!* It must be that he had found the cave and taken shelter there. Probably he was not a Campbell, then, but more likely hiding from them— though he would not stay hidden long, with the smoke giving him away. Kelpie grinned sourly and shrugged. This was no place for her, then. She turned and prepared to slip quietly away, back to the shieling.

"And have I taken the home of the water witch?"

It was a low voice with a mocking note that Kelpie could never mistake. She whirled. Alex! She could see him now through the brush, nearly invisible against the low winter sun. He sat at the mouth of a small, shallow cave, regarding her quizzically—but with a drawn look about the mouth of him. One foot, badly swollen, was propped up before him.

Och, then, wasn't it her curse on him that had come at last to bear fruit? Moving thru the juniper, but keeping a safe distance away, Kelpie told him so with considerable relish.

Alex grinned wryly. "It may be so," he conceded. "Sure it is you've cursed me enough. But have I not told you that such things are likely to fly back in the face of the one who curses? And if this is your curse at work, then 'tis not just me you've harmed, but Montrose and his army, and yourself as well. For Argyll is about, and I was on my way up the Great Glen to warn Montrose when I fell; and what will you do if Argyll wins and puts his witch-hunters over the whole of the Highlands?"

His tone was still mocking, but Kelpie could hear bitterness and despair in his voice. It made her feel most peculiar, for Alex was usually so infuriatingly self-assured—and much easier to hate that way. His distress was not quite as satisfying as it should have been. For a moment she toyed with the idea of leaving him to his worry, but she could not resist bragging. She gave him a pointed grin.

"You will always be thinking yourself the only clever body in the world," she observed smugly. "I myself have already sent a messenger to Montrose."

Alex stared, frankly unbelieving. "You?"

"And why not, whatever? Wasn't I crossing Campbell land myself with the army, and you away safe out of it? Haven't I the wits to see I'm not wanting Mac Cailein Mor king in the Highlands? It is I should be doubting you, for if Ian and his father are with Montrose now, I'm thinking you'd not be going near whatever."

Alex narrowed his hazel eyes at her, and Kelpie prudently moved a step farther away. "And why not?" he inquired lazily.

Kelpie laughed nastily. "I've eyes in my head!" she retorted. "Did you think I was not seeing? Aye, and I saw it before, as well, with the Second Sight, last spring."

Alex's eyes widened for an instant, then narrowed. He seemed about to say something, but changed his mind. Instead, the planes in his face became more angular than ever, and he gave Kelpie a long, hard, brooding stare that made her thankful for the hurt foot which kept him from moving. For surely he was thinking that he would like to silence her. He shrugged finally. "I wonder," he said, "whether 'tis the truth you're telling me about that messenger. If so, I could find it in my heart . . ."

He didn't finish the thought, nor did Kelpie answer. Instead, she stared back at him, at the freckles and straight lines of his face, at the way the cheekbones stood out above the narrow strength of jaw, and at the tangled red hair which had not been trimmed or combed recently. He was thinner than he had been and pale under his freckles, and she could see a tiny pulse in his temple that was his life itself—so easy to stop, so small a thread of life. And was there not something she should be doing the now, to avenge Ian? But she could not think what. Alex was not asleep, nor by any means helpless, even with a sore foot; and she had no intention at all of risking her own life for Ian or anyone else. She pulled her thick brows together and regarded him darkly.

Alex laughed suddenly. "You cannot be planning to rob me, so it must be some other devilment you have in mind. Are you not satisfied yet, water witch? Is it another wee spell, or have you learned the Evil Eye by now?"

"Sssss!" said Kelpie earnestly.

"Well, and why will you not be going to Mac Cailein Mor to say that I am here?" he asked. "He would make short enough shrift of me, and would you not be liking that?"

"Aye so," agreed Kelpie with enthusiasm. "But," she pointed out regretfully, "he would be making even shorter shrift of me, and I'd not be liking that so well." And then she bit her tongue in annoyance as Alex laughed again. It was a spell he had put on her, to be always telling him the truth she had never intended to say!

She scowled and lifted her lip in the old wolfish snarl, and then found herself grinning ruefully, though she had never intended that, either. It was not funny; it was *not!* She stamped her foot.

"Ou, aye!" said Alex. "Your sense of humor has slipped out again, and why will you be squashing it under? Laugh at yourself, Kelpie. 'Tis the cure for all ills, and it is in my mind that perhaps most evil is caused by folk who take themselves too seriously."

"You're daft," said Kelpie and turned away uncertainly. She should be off about her business and leave Alex to his fate. But it seemed that the thing inside that had been pushing her for days against her will was pushing still. It was as if she were living a pattern, and it was yet unfinished, and the thing would not permit her to go off and leave it until it was complete. She paused, her back turned to Alex, who sat still and silent in the mouth of his refuge.

"What will you be doing now?" she asked against her will.

"Bide here," he returned philosophically, "since I can do nothing else, and see what will happen."

"They will be seeing your smoke," she pointed out, still reluctantly.

"I will let my fire die during the day, and try to keep warm by moving about," he returned, and the quizzical note was back in his voice. "And why do you warn me of that, water witch? Wouldn't it please you just to see me captured?"

"It would that!" Kelpie's eyes flashed. "I will be laughing that day, and not at myself either!" And this time she did leave, heading angrily back toward the Spean River.

20. The Campbell Lass

KELPIE went back to the hut, since there was no other shelter and it was better to risk Campbells than to freeze to death. But she found a hiding place on the river bank, just in case, and for three days she alternately huddled over the tiny coals which were all she dared have during the daytime and watched the path for signs of the invaders.

There was plenty of time to think. She wondered whether the message had got through to Montrose, and what he could do even if it had. For he was trapped in the Great Glen between two armies, and no way out except over mountains impassable with snow. She wondered about Alex and that long, inscrutable look he had given her, and it came to her that she had been a fool to tell him that she knew what he had done. For if he could strike down his foster brother, it would be nothing for him to silence her. She began to feel very trapped herself. Was no place in the world safe for her?

Lost in brooding, she failed to keep her sharp watch, and on the third afternoon she heard, too late, the crunch of heavy steps in the crusted snow. Before she could do more than turn, a heavy-set Campbell flung the door open, two or three others looming behind him.

"Here'll be another cursed Cameron or two," he shouted, and his broadsword bore grim stains from the last house he had visited. "And where is your husband hiding, lass?"

Kelpie's wits, well trained in crisis, worked quickly. "Husband indeed!" she retorted, staring boldly into the ruddy face. "Where are your eyes, man, that you cannot recognize a Campbell when you see one?" She snatched up Lady Argyll's cloak and waved it at him, thankful for that particular theft. "Och, but I am glad that you have come," she went on with a trusting upward smile through her lashes. "It was my wicked Cameron uncle who came by my home on Loch Awe with that devil Montrose and all the army, and stole me away to keep house for him, since his wife died, and he saying I must be his daughter now and some day marry a Cameron; and have I not been biding my time and waiting for warm weather to run away back home?"

The Campbells blinked and believed her. She was utterly convincing, and in any case, what Cameron would have claimed to be a Campbell, even at the edge of death?

And had she not the once fine Campbell cloak, clearly given her by a lady of that clan? The sword went back into its sheath.

"Och, well," said its owner with a sigh. "Naught to do here but burn the place. But at least you can be coming back the now."

This was the last thing Kelpie wanted! "To another army?" she jeered, hiding her panic. "No, now, I've enough of armies and battles. Leave me be, just, and when 'tis warmer I'll be finding my own way. Will you not be fighting Montrose soon?" she demanded. "Or is it only women and bairns you are after?"

They shuffled their feet. "We'll be taking care of Montrose," promised the stout one. "But we cannot leave you here, lass. You must just come along back to Inverlochy, and perhaps himself will be seeing you're sent back home."

Kelpie's heart threatened to choke her. He'd be sending her back, fine enough! "*Dhé!*" she sputtered, knowing her life might depend on her next words. "Will ye be bothering the likes of him with a nobody, and him with a war on his hands? He'd no be thanking ye for it! Besides," she confided beseechingly, "it is myself am afraid of Mac Cailein Mor, and he so great and all. No, now, just leave me here, and then it's away back I'll be by myself."

The stout one was not unsympathetic. "Well, women have daft fears," he observed. "But 'tis true enough that himself is an awesome man. We cannot leave you here, but perhaps we can be tucking you into a wee bit place near Inverlochy where you'll not be noticed until we move on. There is a burned shieling just near the loch, with one end left untouched. Come along now."

To argue further would be hopeless and perhaps fatal. This was a stubborn man, already close enough to suspicion. Numb with apprehension, Kelpie wrapped the cloak firmly around herself and let them lead her outside while they fired the thatch.

And then, just as they were climbing up the bank, a tall man pointed to a faint wisp of smoke to the southeast. "Another shieling," he announced happily.

It was no shieling at all, of course. It was Alex's fire, and now Kelpie's curse would be well and truly fulfilled. Why hadn't she thought of telling them herself? And why was it that she felt more dismay than elation? Frowning, she probed at the feeling, trying to figure it out. Och, of course; It was not for Alex's sake she did not want him caught, but for her own. For he would be sure to tell them that she was no Campbell at all but a gypsy lass, and then they would take her straight to Argyll. She bit her lip as she silently followed the Campbells up the Cour in the direction of the telltale smoke, hoping passionately that Alex would either get away or be killed before he could betray her.

He nearly did get away. The cave, when they finally found it, was empty, the fire quenched with snow. The

tangled footprints in the snow seemed to lead nowhere,
and they might have given up but for the stubbornness
of Hamish, the stout man. But at last someone saw Alex
hiding high up amid the dark needles of a pine tree.

"A MacDonald!" Hamish peered upward. "Come away
down, now, or we'll shoot you there."

"And what difference?" asked Alex mockingly from his
high perch. "I'd as lief be shot here as on the ground."

Kelpie set her teeth. She hoped they'd shoot him now,
before he could see her and speak against her. She *did!*
But again Hamish had other ideas. What was a MacDonald
doing here at all, he wanted to know, and one, moreover,
who was clearly well educated and therefore at least the
son of a chieftain? It was a thing out of the ordinary and
had better have the attention of his own chieftain, Campbell of Auchinbreck.

"We're no for shooting you now," he announced, "but
will be taking you prisoner."

Alex seemed to think it over for a moment. Then he
laughed. "'Twill be a braw task for you, then," he observed, "for I've a sore hurt ankle and can no longer set
it to the ground—or else you'd not have found me here,
whatever. Are you wanting to carry me all that way? For
if not, you may as well shoot me here."

This last clearly appealed to most of the Campbells,
but Hamish stuck out his jaw. "Aye, then. Finlay and

Angus will carry you," he announced, to the displeasure of two of his men.

Alex shrugged and came down, leaning for an instant against the trunk of the tree as he reached the ground. His face was cool, although his ankle must be hurting him badly. But his lips tightened slightly when he saw Kelpie, and he stood for an instant, fixing her with another of those long, penetrating looks. There was more than mockery in it now. Kelpie flinched from it, and it came to her that Alex thought she had brought the Campbells to find him.

Of course he did! How could he suppose anything else? And he knew quite well that he held the power of vengeance in his own tongue. For although he could not know what was between Kelpie and Mac Cailein Mor, the mere word "witch" would be quite enough to destroy her.

She waited for it, head high, with the look of a trapped fox in her eyes, hoping they might kill her swiftly, for Argyll would do worse. But Alex did not say it. Looking into her eyes, he gave one short contemptuous laugh and turned away. And while he arranged himself in the hand-chair made by the reluctant Finlay and Angus, Kelpie stood quite still, hot and shaken by feelings she hadn't known she possessed.

She tried to collect her thoughts during the long, slow trip back to Inverlochy Castle. Why had Alex not denounced her? He must be waiting, knowing she would be tormented by uncertainty. He would do it, doubtless, when they reached the castle. Och, then, she must forget the searing pain of his laughter, and try to get away!

Dusk was lowering as they neared Inverlochy, and she sidled up to walk alongside Hamish. "I am frightened," she whispered pathetically. "There are too many men, and I used to the lonely hills and cattle. Can I not just be slipping away down the loch and home? I know the way well enough."

He looked at her kindly. "No, 'tis much too cold for you to be traveling alone," he said with firmness.

Kelpie's lip trembled—and for this she required no great dramatic ability, either. He looked alarmed. "Do not be crying, now," he said hastily. "I tell you, I know a place where you can bide, and no need to be going among the army at all. Just wait now until I'm turning the prisoner over to Auchinbreck. Fergus, run ahead a bit and see can you find out where he is the now."

He clasped Kelpie's cold hand firmly in his, no doubt thinking he was comforting her; and Kelpie had to trudge along beside him, her heart thudding with fear. It thudded harder when Fergus returned to report that Auchinbreck was away down at the loch with Mac Cailein Mor, seeing about the two cannon.

"Fine, then," said Hamish. "For the wee bit placie for you to hide is down there too, and we need not be going near the castle at all but just deliver the prisoner and ask can you stay there at the same time." And he beamed heartily upon the quaking Kelpie, who saw no escape now from a witch's death by fire.

Setting her teeth hard upon her lower lip, she tried to remember that she had faced death before. But this time she seemed to have no courage in reserve. The long strain had drained it from her. She could only remember Mac Cailein Mor's cruel face and unbearable dungeon, and think that this could not really be happening, and wish that she could drop dead on the spot and be done with it.

They were just past the castle now, and Hamish turned to watch a scattered group of soldiers come running from the slopes of Ben Nevis, cutting behind his group, in a great hurry to reach the castle. There was an air of alarm in their gray shapes in the dusk, and Hamish stared after them curiously.

"A fine hurry they are in," he said. "I wonder what news it is they are bringing from the ben, and what they could be finding at all on that wild place."

"Perhaps the water-bull of Lundavra has been straying north a bit," suggested Alex, breaking his long silence. His voice dropped to an eerie whisper, and only Kelpie could hear the hint of laughter in it. "You'll have heard of it, no doubt, with its broad ears and black hoofs and wild demon eye?"

The soldiers shivered, and one made a gesture, quickly halted, of crossing himself. For though the Campbells were now all good members of the Kirk, old habits remained from many generations past and were likely to pop up in a crisis.

They went on, with occasional furtive glances over their shoulders at the brooding shape of that giant mountain Ben Nevis—the highest, it was said, in all of the British Isles, and therefore an apt place for uncanny and ungodly things. Kelpie too would have been glad to scurry from its menace, had there not been a greater one facing her. As it was, she would gladly have fled to Ben Nevis for protection, even if there were a dozen water-bulls there.

They had circled below the castle now, to the river, and were perhaps a mile from Loch Linnhe. If only Hamish would relax his hard, reassuring grip on her hand, she might be able to dive into the surrounding dusk and lose herself. But when she gently tested his grip, he merely tightened it.

Perhaps if she should suggest to him that she could walk better with both hands free? Or was it already too late? There was a group of dark shapes in the gloom just ahead now. If that was Argyll, this was her last chance! "Please," she began in her softest voice, and got no further.

From behind came the pound of running footsteps, and an excited voice raised. "Mac Cailein Mor! Mac Cailein Mor!"

A soldier rushed past them to the figures a few yards ahead, and the cold voice of Argyll answered. "Here. What is it, then?"

"Montrose!" The soldier gasped. "Some of our scouts have just come back. They say Montrose is on Ben Nevis!"

21. Vengeance

IN THE shocked silence which followed, Hamish forgot
his comforting grip on the poor wee frightened lass for
an instant, and in that instant the poor wee frightened
lass vanished.

She crouched on the far side of a rhododendron bush,
tensed and ready for further flight. For the moment, it
was best not to move again, for there was silence beside
the river, and she dared make no noise that might call
attention to herself. Och, the good luck of it! And a fine
chance there was that, with this news, no one would think
of her again at all.

"Impossible!" said Argyll. His voice was thin.

"It is true, Mac Cailein Mor!" insisted the messenger.
"On the north slope of Ben Nevis it was, his army ran
into our outpost, and some of our scouts escaped and
came to warn us."

"Impossible," repeated Argyll more thinly yet. "He

couldn't. He went up the Great Glen, and he hasn't come back down it. And there's no other way he could have come in this cold and snow—not with an army and horses and cannon. It's not humanly possible."

There was a good deal of sense in this. Even Kelpie, still as a bogle behind her bush, frowned in puzzlement. How *could* Montrose have come so quickly, and *not* through the Great Glen? Over the bitter impassable mountains, then? Och, Glen Roy, it must be! Argyll didn't know this country as she did, and as the Camerons and Mac-Donalds would. Through Glen Roy, then—and it was next to impossible even then, but if anyone at all could do it, then it would be Montrose and his Highlanders, and she the cause of it all, with her message! She hugged herself silently.

"It couldna be the army," said an Edinburgh voice soothingly. "Gin 'tis Montrose at all, which I doot, 'tis a mere handfu' o' wild Hieland thieves he could ha' brought, and we'll wipe 'em oot the morn."

"Still and all," came another voice, "it might be best for you to be going on board your galley, your Lordship. You've an injured shoulder, remember, and you're too valuable to risk your life in a mere skirmish."

"You may be right." There was unmistakable relief in Argyll's voice, and Kelpie lifted her short lip in contempt. "I can put you in charge, Auchinbreck, and send commands from my galley. Who is that over there?"

His voice rose sharply, and Kelpie's hair stood on end until she heard Hamish's apologetic answer. "Hamish Campbell, just, with a MacDonald I found skulking up near the Spean River, and I thinking you might be wanting to see him."

"A MacDonald?" Auchinbreck's voice was incisive. "Aye, he's likely a scout for Montrose and may be able to tell us something. Will you speak to him, Your lordship?"

"Later," said Argyll. "Take him down to the shelter by the loch and stay there yourselves on guard. See that no one goes near the galley, and I'll question the prisoner before I go board."

There was a crunch of snow as Argyll and his party started back toward the castle, and then a pause. "Why isn't he tied?" came Argyll's voice accusingly.

"Och, your Lordship, he has a hurt foot, and it would be too hard to carry him this whole way if—"

"He could have been shamming, you fool!" Argyll was furious. "Tie him now."

He went on, leaving the other group of dark shapes where they stood. "Well, so, and himself was saying 'now,'" muttered Hamish, "so now it is, my lad. We'll have your two hands behind you. *Were* you shamming?"

"Not a whit," said Alex coolly. "I'd have left you before this, if I were."

"Well, I almost have it in my heart to pity you, just for

your courage, though you're a cursed MacDonald. Angus, where's the wee lass?"

"She was off and away at the word Montrose," reported Angus, "and no wonder. She's frighted even of our army and will be in terror of his. She'll no be staying for a battle."

"Och, she'll freeze, just, poor *amadain!*" said Hamish worriedly. "And she could have been staying at the shelter with us, and quite safe. Well, so. Come away now."

They moved off toward the loch, leaving Kelpie to figure out her new situation.

It was a great improvement, surely, but hardly rosy. If only the weather were warm, there would be no problem at all. She could set off for safety, leaving Alex just where she wanted him, and Montrose over behind the mountain to settle with Argyll after Argyll had settled with Alex. But it was cold! And there would be no shelter near, what with all the homes burned. And she didn't want to freeze.

An hour earlier she would gladly have taken the chance, gladly frozen, even, in preference to meeting Argyll. But now that she was out of danger from him for the moment, she wanted to live, and how could she be arranging it? If it were not for Alex, she might slip down to the shelter after all, and just hide when Argyll came. But Alex would not miss another chance to betray her. He had delayed too long once before, and he must be cursing himself for it.

But she had to do something! Shivering, she got to her feet and silently followed an orange glimmer down near the loch. Och, a fire! Kelpie hurried her steps until she could see the ruins of a shieling hut, one side open to the night, but with a warm fire just at the edge, where the fireplace had once stood. Alex, well bound now, was lying against one wall, and the other men were grouped around. As she watched, they began taking food from their pouches.

In an agony of indecision, Kelpie crouched in the bushes, just too far away to feel the warmth of the fire, but she didn't dare to go closer. She could almost wish Alex free, so that—

Her eyes widened. Alex had turned over to face the wall and was unmistakably settling down to sleep! How could he? Reluctantly Kelpie admired him for it. He was a bad one, but for all that he had a cool courage that was fine.

She waited a few minutes more; then she *had* to get warm! And Alex seemed to be truly asleep. Standing up, she raised her voice scarcely above a whisper. "Hamish!"

He was up, his ruddy face turning to search the bushes. "The wee lass! Are you frozen, just? Come away to the fire. It was gey foolish of you to run off."

She came, rubbing her numbed hands in the heavenly warmth, even though it made them hurt sorely. "I was affrighted," she explained, "of Montrose, and of all the men, and of Mac Cailen Mor, and even of him." She nodded toward Alex. "Please, if anyone comes, could I not be hiding away at the back behind the walls until they go?"

"Ou, aye," said Hamish tolerantly, "if you're so frighted as all that."

It was nearly morning, and Kelpie had napped a little herself and was warm and fed (with a wary eye on the sleeping Alex), before voices and steps announced a party coming from the castle. In a flash she was around behind the ruined shieling, just at the corner where she could hear everything and even see a bit. She would be safe enough from now on, for although it was still dark enough to escape, the faintest of gray appeared over the stern dome of Ben Nevis, and the peaks farther south were beginning to show starkly black against the lighter clouds. The night was over, and she could afford to stay and watch what happened to Alex.

"Put my things aboard," ordered Argyll's cold voice. "I'll be along as soon as I see to this prisoner. Where is he?"

"Here, asleep," replied Hamish humbly. "Wake you up, MacDonald! Mac Cailein Mor wants to talk to you."

Apparently Alex awoke as Kelpie always did, all at once, for there was no trace of sleepiness in his voice. "Well, then, and let us talk," he returned casually.

Kelpie knew that his coolness would enrage Argyll, who

repeatedly fled danger and was about to do it again. This would go hard with Alex. She *must* see! There was a hole in the wall, just at the corner, where a stone had fallen out, and surely no one would be noticing a wee eye in the dark!

She applied the eye to the hole. Sure enough, Argyll's pale face was twisted with anger, the habitual sneer deeper than usual. And Alex had that faintly amused smile on his face, despite bound hands and swollen foot, and despite his fear.

"Your name?" asked Argyll harshly.

"Alexander MacDonald of Ardochy on Loch Garry," replied Alex proudly.

"So. Son of a chieftain, then. And what were you doing skulking in Lochaber?"

"Nursing a sprained ankle," replied Alex, still with a faint smile, "and hoping to be overlooked by your men."

"You knew we were here, then?" Argyll pounced upon the idea like a man looking for an excuse to unleash a storm of venom. And there was no doubt he had his victim. Kelpie's revenge would be better than she had ever dreamed! She pressed closer to her peephole to see if Alex's face would betray fear. But he just lifted a sandy eyebrow.

"Could anyone *not* be knowing you were here, with the smoke of burning homes rising like the plague?" he retorted reasonably.

"You are one of Montrose's men!" Argyll said accusingly, and Kelpie found herself thinking of the things Alex might answer to that. He would never claim to be a Covenanter, proud fool that he was, but he could say he was not with Montrose, that he never had been, that he had had a quarrel with the Camerons—any number of things. But he said none of them. Did he not know that his silence would seem an admission of guilt? Kelpie fumed at his stupidity before she remembered that—this time—she was on Argyll's side.

"You are a spy left behind!" Argyll went on threateningly. "It was you warned him we were here!"

"I wish I *had* been the one," confessed Alex wryly. "I would not be here if I had. But since I *am* here, and not with Montrose, that is clearly nonsense."

"Don't quibble with me!" Argyll was in a cold rage, the cruel, bullying streak in him showing clear. "You were responsible. You hurt your foot and sent someone else with the message."

In the gleam of the fire, Alex's jaw moved up and outward a fraction. "I would have done so," he retorted proudly, "but that I could find no one to send."

"You'll not save your life that way." There was wintry satisfaction in Argyll's face. "Unless you can produce the guilty party and prove your innocence . . ." The sentence went grimly unfinished.

Even Hamish looked shocked at this unfairness, and

for an instant Kelpie missed the full irony of the situation. Then it dawned on her. Alex was to die for the thing she herself had done—and he well aware of it and helpless, since he had no notion where she was! It was almost too good to be possible!

She bit her lip and pressed closer to the chink, and a squeak of what must be delight—although it felt almost like a sob—escaped her.

Alex turned—oh, so casually!—and his eyes, dark in the shadow of the shelter, looked straight into hers.

Kelpie stopped breathing. Too appalled even to move, she stood frozen, waiting for the simple, deadly words that must come next. In her mind she heard them clearly. "Very well so, and you will find the guilty party is the witch lass hiding this very moment outside the wall. . . ." She should be away, running like a hare! But she could not, for her shock had glued her feet to the ground, and already Alex had begun to speak.

"And how," he asked deliberately, "could I be doing that?"

Kelpie missed the next part of the conversation, for she was altogether stunned. He had seen and recognized her; never a doubt of it. In that instant she had handed him the victory, his own life and hers as well, and he had dropped them indifferently at his feet! Why? Was he fey, then, to be deliberately throwing away his life? Not even the scruples of Ian could account for it, for Alex owed her nothing and less than nothing, especially since he believed she had betrayed him to the Campbells.

In her bewilderment she didn't even feel relief at her own narrow escape. And when she was again able to concentrate on the scene inside, she found that Alex had taken the edge off her victory simply by giving it to her. Where had the triumph and savor gone? Frowning, she reminded herself that Alex was being justly punished for what he did to Ian, and she was *not* sorry! No, nor would she ever dream of wanting to save him whatever, for he deserved to die, and had she not been planning revenge? She would not *want* to help him even if she could—and couldn't if she wanted to, for was it not her rule of life to look out for herself and no one else? And if Mac Cailein Mor should so much as glimpse the witch lass caught trying to hex him, and herself wearing his own wife's gown and cloak this moment . . . She laughed at herself for even thinking that such a daft idea could ever enter her head. It was gloating she was. She *was!*

Intent on her gloating, she risked another peep through the chink and saw that Argyll was biting his lip with anger. Alex had no doubt just said something derisive, for he was smiling recklessly. But for all his composure, Kelpie knew that he was afraid in the face of death. Had not she herself, more than once, acted calm when she did not feel that way? Och, she knew how his heart must be pounding, as her own was just from imagining it.

Or perhaps it was pounding with happiness and excitement and triumph. Her fists were clenched painfully and her lips drawn back from her teeth. This was the moment, and she would watch while—while—

"Take him out yonder and shoot him," said Argyll.

Then Kelpie heard a reckless laugh coming from her own lips, and she found herself around the wall and in the firelight and confronting Argyll with her head held high.

"No, now," she said, "for 'twas I sent the messenger."

One part of her stood aghast and terrified at the insane thing she had done, but the other part—the thing inside, which had been pushing her for so long—was glad and triumphant.

22. The Last Word

For a moment even the daybreak seemed to pause over the Highlands. The thin sky of morning lighted a wan world of muted gray and white and purple with an eerie, ghostlike tone. There was no sound outside the ruined shelter with its circle of sickly firelight, and for just an instant there was no sound even there.

Alex's face seemed carved in an odd expression of exultation and anguish combined, and his eyes fixed upon her as if they would never leave. But Kelpie did not see this, for her own eyes were fixed defiantly upon Argyll, waiting.

She had not long to wait. "The witch!" he whispered, and his eyes blazed in pale fury. "And in her Ladyship's stolen clothes!" he added with new outrage.

Alex laughed, and his laughter was delighted, exasperated—and somehow sad. He moved to stand beside

Kelpie. "Och," he said, "and isn't it just the way you
will be overdoing things? I would have had you remain
unprincipled and live. I would have called you liar and
saved you yet. But you must appear in Lady Argyll's
stolen clothes and seal your doom—and knowing it!" His
eyes were stricken, exultant, tender; but Kelpie only
looked at him dazedly. All of it was beyond her understanding, except that she had doomed herself irrevocably
by her own madness, and the thing inside said it must be
so.

Argyll was breathing hard, taut with hatred; his menace
was overwhelming. "Shoot the man now," he said between
his teeth, "but bind the witch and take her aboard the
galley. I will try her and burn her when this business with
Montrose is over."

And then all Lochaber seemed to explode at once. Shots
echoed from Ben Nevis just as Alex went quite berserk.
His face was as she had seen it in the witch-hunting town,
jutted with sharp angles of rage. He hurled himself against
Argyll, the full force of his hard shoulder driving into the
Campbell's midsection; and down they went. The others
rushed forward with yells, and from the castle came more
yells and a new volley of shots.

Hamish was pulling his chief from under Alex and
shouting, "The battle has started!" Someone kicked Alex
brutally in the head, and Kelpie flung herself at the culprit,
using both teeth and nails, and was herself flung to the

ground, while still another voice shouted, "Get you to the galley, Mac Cailein Mor!"

Kelpie, dazed from her fall, saw Argyll, staggering and winded, clutching his shoulder and croaking contradictions. "Shoot them! Take the witch on board! I'll burn them both! Shoot them at once!" Alex struggled up and tried to shield Kelpie with his own body as someone raised a gun. She heard a wild shriek of pipes from the direction of Ben Nevis, more shots and more yells. And then came a blaze of pain, and nothing at all.

She lay for a while without opening her eyes, trying to decide whether she was really alive. It seemed quite unlikely. But on the other hand, except for a sore pain in her head and a hot, smoldering one in her body, this did not seem like Hell. For one thing, she seemed to be in a soft bed with sheets, and surely Hell would never provide such things. She decided to open her eyes and find out.

Opening her eyes did not help much, but only added to her confusion. For was not this one of the bedrooms at Glenfern, which she had helped often enough to clean? And whatever could she be doing here at all? Clearly she could not be here—but how was it that a stout and smiling Marsali seemed to be feeding her beef broth? Och, it was too much effort to worry about it! She swallowed the broth, closed her eyes, and slept again. The next time she awoke, it was to morning light, and she felt much stronger.

There was a small movement to the left of the bed, and Kelpie slowly focused her eyes toward it. A flower face lighted and moved closer. "Och, my Kelpie!" whispered Wee Mairi, radiant. "You've come away back to me!"

Hot tears stung Kelpie's eyes. She closed them and moved her left hand gropingly and felt a small warm one creep into it. Och, the wee love! The tears slid down her cheeks.

There was more movement presently, and then Ronald's voice asking with deep interest, "Is she awake yet?"

"Of course she is, or how else could she be weeping?" demanded his twin scornfully. "Kelpie, is it hurting you are? Can you open your eyes, Kelpie? Fiona, will you run to tell Mother she is awake?"

Kelpie opened her eyes mistily and saw the rosy, concerned faces over her. Fiona, crossing herself as usual, appeared beyond them and then disappeared again. Donald vanished too, while Kelpie—still gripping Wee Mairi's hand—closed her eyes again and tried to sort out the confusion of her thoughts. Presently there was a slight denting of the bed near her elbow.

"I've brought Dubh," announced Donald cheerfully. "We decided before that you were not a witch, but now Alex says you are, but a nice one; and I was thinking, if Dubh is still liking you, perhaps Alex is right."

Kelpie wrinkled her forehead as Dubh spat nastily at Donald. Alex? Alex at Glenfern? Dubh regarded her with slitted yellow eyes and then draped himself in a scraggy, purring fur piece across her shoulder. "Alex?" said Kelpie aloud, puzzled.

"Ou, aye, and he sore hurt, too." Ronald nodded. "But he is better now. Kelpie, when you are well, will you tell us about your adventures? Why were you leaving Glenfern at all, Kelpie? Do you *like* your Grannie Witchie, or was it that you were afraid of her, as Father said? Is she truly a witch, Kelpie? Where is she the now? Are you going to stay with us? Wee Mairi says you love her. Do you, Kelpie?"

The small hand in Kelpie's stirred. "Aye so!" piped Wee Mairi indignantly. "My Kelpie *does* love me!"

"Aye," confessed Kelpie, her defenses quite down. "But," she went on incredulously, "is Alex truly here? At Glenfern?"

"Of course," said Donald. "He has been telling us of his adventures too, and how Montrose was sending him on a special important mission to talk to clan chiefs and see if Lochiel would join the army, and all; and that was why he was alone and caught by the Campbells. But we do not know why you were there at all." He paused, head tilted hopefully to one side.

But Kelpie, more and more bewildered, was in no state to tell stories. "Alex?" she repeated stupidly.

"Himself." It was his voice, with something new in the laughter of it. Suddenly the room was full of people.

Eithne and Lady Glenfern smiled at her from the foot of the bed, and Alex himself was coming slowly across the floor. There was a bandage round his head, and he leaned heavily on Glenfern and Ian.

Och, it made no sense at all! Kelpie closed her eyes again and moved her head fretfully.

"Alex has told us what you did," said Glenfern. "It is at such times that a person's true character comes forth." He smiled down at her warmly. "Let you know now, Kelpie, that you will always have a home at Glenfern, and our love; and for saving Alex we owe you a debt that we can never pay."

Kelpie's puzzlement deepened. *Dhé!* It must be that Ian had never known that it was Alex who struck him down! In the confusion, perhaps herself was the only one who had really seen it. It must be so, for no other explanation made sense. Perhaps Archie hadn't known either, and she had merely read meanings into his words that evening in the camp. Her blue eyes flew open and met Alex's quizzical ones. What an actor he was, then, behaving as if nothing had happened! But *she* could tell them what had happened, and Alex knew it, and yet here he stood quite at ease.

They stared at each other for a long, searching moment, and a look of baffled frustration came to both faces. And then Kelpie closed her eyes once again, too weak to cope with such a puzzle or even to decide whether or no she should tell Ian what his foster brother had done.

"*Dhé*, and she'll be confused enough, poor water witch!" The old teasing note in Alex's voice overlaid a new tenderness. "Just be settling me in a chair by the bed, and then away out, the rest of you, whilst I tell her the end of our adventure."

Presently the room was silent again, except for Dubh's purring. Conscious of a presence beside the bed, Kelpie opened a cautious eye again after a minute and found the hazel eyes fixed on her broodingly.

"Och so," he murmured, shaking his head sadly. "I had thought my cousin Cecily unpredictable and you an open book, with your devious wiles, and so candidly unprincipled. And then—you put a spell on me, with the ringed witch-eyes in your head. You baffled me, you haunted me, you eluded me, leaving me forever two jumps behind and never knowing what to think at all. Aye me, I suppose I shall never understand you at all, and that is my fate and destiny."

Kelpie slowly progressed from bewilderment to indignation. Only the last words had any meaning whatever, and that was little enough.

"*I!*" she fumed, causing Dubh to dig in a protesting claw. "It is you who make no sense at all, and I never knowing what to think!"

Alex grinned ruefully. "At least we are even, then. Are you wanting to know what has happened since Argyll's men put bullets in the both of us?"

Kelpie nodded.

"Well, then, were you hearing the start of the battle, just as our own wee war was getting exciting?" asked Alex. She nodded again, content to lie still and listen. "Well," he went on, "it was the battle that saved us, for Argyll rushed off to the safety of his galley, and his men left us for dead—and very nearly right they were. And so we lay unknowing while Montrose won a great victory over an army twice his size. It was another Tippermuir, and this time the fighting force of the Campbells is crippled for years to come. Some say as many as fifteen hundred were slain, and the rest taken prisoner or chased back to their own country, and our men on their heels all the way to Lundavra. I think it will be another generation, Kelpie, before Clan Campbell can come raiding other clans again —and a good blow for the King's cause as well," he added, almost as an afterthought. Loyal to the king though he was, Alex was a Highlander, and Highland affairs were his closest concern.

Kelpie found herself wondering suddenly about Morag Mhor and Rab, Archie, and the others. "And had we many killed?"

Alex shook his head. "It was a rout," he said. "They tell me there are some two hundred or more wounded, but

scarce over a dozen killed outright. It seems fair unbeliev-
able."

Kelpie assimilated this and then returned to another
matter of interest. "What of Mac Cailein Mor?" she demanded vindictively. "And what was happening to us,
after all?"

"Och, the great General Campbell was away down the
loch in his galley before the fight was yet over, hero that
he is!" Scorn was bright in Alex's voice. "But as for us,
we lay until some of our men found us and recognized my
tartan, so they took us up to the castle with the other
wounded. There were plenty of the army who knew me
—and you, too, it seems, for there was a hulking great
man named Rab and a huge fierce woman called Morag
Mhor nearly come to blows over which could be doing
most for you." His eyes crinkled at her with approval and
amusement. "So it was soon enough that my brother and
Ian both found us. And when we were fit to be carried,
they brought us here."

"Here!" echoed Kelpie, renewed bafflement upon her.
Forgetting her wounds, she tried to sit up and then
changed her mind. Wincing, she lay back again, and her
ringed eyes stared beneath lowered brows at Alex. Dubh,
his nap disturbed, glared with equal fierceness, and Alex
found the combination disconcerting.

"You would be coming *here?*" Kelpie spat. "You, with
all your prating of loyalty and the laws of hospitality

and this principles thing? And you have not even good sense, for here am I, and whatever makes you think I will not be telling? And yet you have not even tried to threaten me."

Complete bewilderment was on Alex's face. "Either your wits or mine are wandering entirely," he said. "What are you talking about? Tell what?"

"That you tried to kill Ian!" answered Kelpie.

"*What?*" He was utterly dumfounded, and Kelpie's conviction wavered, but only briefly. She knew what she had seen!

"Do not be denying it, for I saw it myself, and twice over—once with the Second Sight, which never lies, and again when it happened."

Alex's eyes narrowed thoughtfully, as if he had begun to see a clue to some deep puzzle. "You were saying something of the sort back at yon cave," he said. "It made no sense, but I had already given up expecting to understand you, and there were other urgent matters on my mind. Tell me now: What was it that you saw twice over? Tell me exactly, for although the Second Sight never lies, sometimes the reading of it can be wrong. What was it you were seeing, water witch?"

Kelpie frowned. "It was the crowd of witch-hunters, although the first time I did not know who or where, or that it was me they were going to burn. But I saw Ian coming through them, and you after him with a black anger on your face. And when you reached him, you raised your sword and brought it down on him, and he dropped like a stone and out of sight." She glared at him defiantly.

A whole series of expressions chased one another across Alex's face, but they were not quite the ones Kelpie had expected. Wonder and relief and joy surely had no place there!

"My sorrow," he whispered, closing his eyes for an instant. "And is it for that you've hated me so darkly this long while? No wonder!" He looked at her suddenly with new delight. "And for Ian too, though you tried so hard to admit no loyalty or friendship, and I believed you! Think carefully," he commanded as Kelpie was about to burst out at him in frustration and fury. "Were you actually *seeing* my sword *strike* Ian?"

"Aye so—" began Kelpie hotly, and then paused. "Well, and there was a head in the way for a wee moment," she conceded, conjuring up the vivid picture and looking at it carefully. "Your sword is striking him just behind the head—the other head, I mean—but now Ian is falling straight away, and so—"

"Look again!" interrupted Alex. "Look closely, Kelpie, and do not judge too quickly. For my sword was falling on the man who was in the act of dirking Ian, and they went down at the same moment. Little *amadain,* how could you be thinking I would turn on my foster brother, dearer than kin, for whom I would give my heart's blood?"

Kelpie scowled in sudden, unreasoning resentment, but he leaned forward to place his hand on her arm where it lay outside the covers. "Look in your heart for the truth," he commanded urgently. "Ask it of your reason as well. You *must* know that I did not do it."

It was true. She did know it. She felt slightly dizzy, as if the sun had spun round suddenly and begun rising in the west. And was it a mistake that she had hated Alex this long time? Och, no! Had he not always infuriated her with his mockery and scorn and his uncanny knowledge of what she would think and do next? But whatever had possessed the both of them that dawn in the shelter, each offering his own life to save the other? She could hardly believe that it had really happened.

The eyes she raised to Alex were night-blue with wonder. "You knew I was hiding behind the wall! Why didn't you save yourself by telling Mac Cailein Mor it was I sent the message? And especially when you thought that I had betrayed you to the Campbells? *Why?*"

There was sudden gladness on Alex's lean face. "Kelpie!" he fairly shouted. "You didn't betray me, then?"

She shook her head irritably and immediately wished she hadn't. "I *told* you I did not dare! And now you know why, with Mac Cailein Mor already wanting me for a witch, and I with his wife's clothing on my back. 'Twas the smoke from your fire betrayed you, fool that you were!" She glared at him. "But you were *believing* it was I, and you needing only a word to save yourself and settle all accounts. Why did you not tell?" she demanded angrily.

Alex grinned flippantly at her, but the angles of his face seemed softened, and his voice as well. He seemed to be laughing at her and at himself too. "Perhaps, *mo chridhe,* it was for the same reason that you spoke out when you needed only to stay still. Can you answer me your own question, Kelpie? Why did you come forth?"

"I was daft, just!" she retorted promptly. "And," she added, remembering, "there was a thing in me pushing where I was not wanting to go." She frowned.

"There has been a thing in me too, this long while," said Alex softly, and for an instant he saw her as she had appeared from the shadows to face Argyll—intense then too, but heartbreakingly brave, nearly tearing him apart with joy for her gallantry and with despair for its result. And he had not known, then, the full horror of what she was facing, that she was giving herself up to be burned as a witch.

She was regarding him with annoyance. "I think it was a spell, whatever," she announced accusingly.

Alex looked at her oddly. "Aye so, a spell," he muttered with a wry twist to his mouth. "And I with a fondness for merry, fair-haired lassies, like my sweet Cecily in Oxford.

And now she will have to marry Ian, just, though perhaps neither of them will mind much. I have *never* cared for witches!" he told her plaintively. "And especially not black-haired ones, with dark, pointy faces, all uncanny eyes. It's never a moment's peace I shall have again; but 'tis a terrible, strong spell you have put on me, and I cannot break it. Och, there's no way at all out of it, but I shall have to marry you, just!"

"Marry me!" Kelpie's shock reached to the very soles of her feet.

"Ou, aye," answered the outrageous lad, wagging his head sadly. "And a dreadful life it will be, never a doubt of it, wed to a wild wee water witch. But marry you I must, for I cannot help myself."

"*I* can, then!" Kelpie sizzled with outrage. "Did you never think of consulting *me*? Were you thinking I would —*Dhé!* I'd sooner be wedding the sea horse in Loch Ness, or Argyll himself! And the very conceit of you to be thinking it! 'Tis a spell indeed I'll be putting on you! Wait until I learn the Evil Eye, and then see will you not be begging my mercy, and with the horrid spots all over you, and—"

Alex silenced her by the simple expedient of putting his lips firmly over hers. When at last he lifted them, it was to laugh into her startled and indignant eyes with the old mockery.

"I'm thinking," he said, just as if she had never uttered a word of her last speech, "that I shall have to be taking you out of Scotland altogether, or sooner or later it would be to the stake with the both of us. And in any case, what else could I be doing with the gypsy wanderlust in your feet?"

"The gypsies *stole* me, I tell you!" retorted Kelpie automatically.

He raised a quizzical eyebrow. "And did they so, truly? Well, and what does it matter? You could never be finding your parents now, nor fit into their life if you did. And in any case, you're going to marry me, and we'll away to the New World. A grand wilderness it is, they say, with all the space needed for wandering in and out of trouble."

He bent toward her again, and reached for her hand, as Kelpie opened a mutinous mouth. Dubh, who had patiently endured the last disturbance of his nap, opened one yellow eye, saw Alex's hand approaching, and slashed it. Then he rearranged himself across Kelpie's neck and went back to sleep.

Kelpie laughed at Alex, who was also laughing and sucking at his torn finger. "You see?" he said. "The Red Indians and wild animals will never have a chance against you with your dark power over man and beast, witch that you are. I wonder, would next week be too soon for the wedding?"

"Sssss!" said Kelpie contentedly.